A love song in the making..

He was her high school sweetheart, the man Candy once dreamed of sharing her life with. But Ty was also a rock star on the rise with a flock of pretty groupies lining up to share his bed. So what makes Ty think that now that he's ready to settle down, Candy will be his one and only? These days the single mom is older and wiser. Still, Candy can't help but feel a stir of something at his hot pursuit....

Ty knows he's got a lot to prove when it comes to winning Candy back. But his rambling, rocker lifestyle has also shown him that she's a woman worth fighting for. No one has ever come close to captivating him the way she did from the first day they met, a sweet-faced young beauty who brought out his every protective instinct. That's why when Candy's family is in crisis, he's willing to risk everything for the woman he's never stopped loving....

Books by Christa Maurice

Drawn to the Rhythm
Satellite of Love
Heaven Beside You
Waiting For A Girl Like You
Let Me Be the One
Not Second Best
Keep Coming Back to Love

Arden FD Three Alarm Tenant
Struck By Lightning
Spark of Desire

Weaver's Circle
Secrets Everybody Knows
Long Memory

One Ring to Rule
Melody Unchained

Published by Kensington Publishing Corporation

Keep Coming Back to Love

A Drawn to the Rhythm Novel

Christa Maurice

LYRICAL PRESS
Kensington Publishing Corp.
www.kensingtonbooks.com

Lyrical Press books are published by
Kensington Publishing Corp. 119 West 40th Street New York, NY 10018

All Kensington titles, imprints, and distributed lines are available at special quantity discounts for bulk purchases for sales promotion, premiums, fund-raising, and educational or institutional use.

To the extent that the image or images on the cover of this book depict a person or persons, such person or persons are merely models, and are not intended to portray any character or characters featured in the book.

Special book excerpts or customized printings can also be created to fit specific needs. For details, write or phone the office of the Kensington Special Sales Manager:
Kensington Publishing Corp.
119 West 40th Street
New York, NY 10018
Attn. Special Sales Department. Phone: 1-800-221-2647.

Kensington and the K logo Reg. U.S. Pat. & TM Off.
LYRICAL PRESS Reg. U.S. Pat. & TM Off.
Lyrical Press and the L logo are trademarks of Kensington Publishing Corp.

First Electronic Edition: November 2016
eISBN-13: 978-1-61650-534-9
eISBN-10: 1-61650-534-6

First Print Edition: November 2016
ISBN-13: 978-1-60183-817-9
ISBN-10: 1-60183-817-4

Printed in the United States of America

Chapter 1

Candy leaned on the cash desk and studied the burnout roaming her section. Seventeen or eighteen, torn-up jeans, concert T-shirt under a black and red flannel, scraggly dirty blond hair, looked as if he hadn't had a decent meal in weeks. A walking cliché. But there was potential.

With a little bit of working out, his too-thin body would be hot. A decent haircut would show off his sweet face. Gawd, those jeans. When they were new, they'd been totally the wrong cut for him. The grease stains and holes weren't helping. He picked up a shirt from a sales rack. Flannel. *Quelle surprise.* A serious Seattle special. He had all the high points of grunge chic but none of the subtleties. Candy scanned the rest of her section. Not a soul. Four-thirty on Thursday was not a big shopping time, and she had thirty minutes before her break. Plenty of time for a project.

"Hi." She smiled and folded her arms behind her back to push her boobs forward. Thanks to the pose and tight shirts, she had the top sales for this section three quarters in a row. If she could keep ahead of that bitch in juniors, she'd win the five-hundred-dollar prize for top sales in the store. Burnout here wasn't going to contribute much, but every little bit helped.

"Hey." He grinned and it lit up his blue eyes.

Oh yeah, this guy had loads of potential, but what the fuck was he trying to do to his hair? Bleach *all* the color out of it? Straw had more sheen. "You need help finding something?"

"I suck at this." He studied the shirt in his hand. "I'm auditioning for this band tonight and I want to look good."

"Okay. What band? Anybody I've heard of?"

"Touchstone."

Touchstone. Candy kept her mouth from dropping open by clenching her teeth. They were hot. Musically anyway. Every one of them could be totally adorable if somebody would invest ten minutes in dressing them right, too. "They're good."

"I know."

"What are you auditioning for?"

"Singer. Jason's been singing since they kicked out their last guy. I really need to look good for this. My mom gave me her credit card, but she's got conferences tonight so she couldn't come help me. I have her phone number at school if you need to call and check." He pulled a store credit card out of his pocket and flashed it before stuffing it back in.

Credit card. Maybe he could help out her sales. Company policy required the cardholder be present, but he did have the number. "No offense, but I don't think your mom is going to help you look good enough to front a band. I bet I can."

His gaze ran over her. Male hormones were her greatest sales aid. A low-cut top and a skirt that was really an inch too short for the store's dress code, but her manager wasn't complaining. Neither was this victim. "Great."

"First, I've got to get you out of those shitty jeans."

He grinned. "Best thing I've heard all day, uh—" He leaned down and looked at her badge. "Candy."

"All right rock star, let's start with these." She handed him a pair of jeans that would accent his long skinny legs in all the right ways and headed toward the shirts.

"How do you know this is my size?"

"I measured you with my eyes." She sent him a flirty grin over her shoulder. Three months ago the store had gotten a shipment of button-down shirts, some with pinstripes, some solid. The solids had flown out the door, but the stripes were piled at the edge of the sale table in the back of the section. Their time had come. A cotton button-down shirt would look striking. Something to show off what body he did have instead of drowning it in flannel. Nice vertical stripes with the narrow-legged jeans would make him look taller, too. Kind of early David Bowie. "You need something a little more impressive on top, too. This flannel thing is so yuck."

"Really? All the big bands dress like this." He plucked at his shirt.

"It doesn't do you any favors. Let's try you in this." She shook the wrinkles from a dark blue shirt with mint green pinstripes. A little odd or distinctive? If his hair was colored to a decent blond, it would be perfect.

Jody was working at the store's salon tonight. "How long do you have before the audition?"

"I have to be there at seven."

Candy made a show of checking her watch. "How much of a makeover do you want to do today?"

His eyes narrowed on her. "Whatever it's gonna take to get into this band."

"Do you trust me?"

"I just met you."

Candy shrugged. "Do you trust me?"

For a long time, he stared at her. She could see the calculations running through his head. How much he needed to win this audition. How little he knew about dressing himself to look good enough to front a hot band. How cute she was. If he had any chance of getting in her pants. That was always a factor. "I trust you. If you get me into this band, I'll take you out."

Yep, how cute she was. That little glimmer of swagger could be nursed to a full-blown inferno if she played him right. "It's a date. You go try that stuff on and I'll call my friend at the salon."

"This isn't gonna cost a lot, is it? My mom will shit if I run up her bill."

So much for improving her sales. "Don't worry. Jody will give you the friend-of-a-friend discount."

"Super." The guy bounded off toward the dressing rooms. Lots of potential.

Once he'd turned through the door, she went to the cash desk and called Jody. "Hey, what are you doing this afternoon?"

"Fuck all. Literally, right now there's a blue-haired old lady getting a perm and three empty chairs. As soon as I'm done with cosmetology school, I am outta here. What about you?"

Candy stared in the direction of the dressing rooms. "I have a challenge for you."

"Really?"

"This guy walked into my section. He's auditioning for Touchstone tonight."

"No way! I love them. He trying out for Max Terry's spot?"

"I don't know."

"What's this guy look like?"

Candy frowned. "That's kinda the problem. The potential is there, but he's screwed up his hair and he looks like he buys his clothes from the Salvation Army while wearing a blindfold."

"He's auditioning tonight?"

"Seven o'clock."

"Plenty of time. You get him dressed and I'll sort out the hair. Can he sing?"

"I have no idea."

"Send him over anyway. I'm bored."

The guy stepped out of the dressing room. Her breath caught. Day for night difference. Tall, lean. Suddenly he had enough presence to walk in front of an audience armed with nothing but a microphone and attitude. Talk about hiding a light under a bushel. He scanned the section. When he saw her, his face brightened and he headed toward her. "You'll need to do something about his face, too. His skin's screwed up way beyond what a little foundation will fix."

"That's not going to happen by seven o'clock."

"I know, but you can start him in the right direction. We want him to look good when he hits the stage with the band."

"Gina's good at that."

"Great. I told him you'd cut him a break on the price."

"He gets in this band, I'll cut his fucking hair for free."

"I'll send him along when I'm done. See ya." Candy hung up the phone. "That looks great."

"Really? I thought it looked fruity." He tugged at the sleeves.

"First of all, you don't tuck it in." She pulled the tails of the shirt out of his pants, letting her fingers brush against his skin. Nice. "These colors are dramatic and bring out your eyes. If you're going to be the lead singer, you have to command people's attention so you have to look good."

He smoothed his hands over the shirt. "It fits."

Candy led him to a mirror and stood behind him. "It would be better if it were taken in a little on the sides." She gathered the material between her fingers. Gawd, he was hot. "You probably don't have time to get to a tailor."

"A tailor?" His eyes went wide.

"Clothes always look better when they're fitted to you."

He turned around and slid his hands down her arms, studying her face. "Is that why yours look so great?"

"Yeah. I tailor all my own clothes."

"And I thought it was the amazing body in them."

Candy curled one side of her mouth into a smile. "That helps, but the clothes accent it."

He pulled her closer. "How do you know all this stuff?"

"I'm going to study fashion merchandising in college." Not only was he hot, he was warm. Lean and firm. Might be the clothes, might be the boy in them, but he had charisma.

"You're in college?"

"No, but after I graduate." She licked her lips. Once Jody took care of his hair and Gina got his skin straightened out, he'd be way beyond cute. "So I called my friend and she's calling out the cavalry to get you set up. We've got the visual end covered, but can you sing?"

He smiled slowly and then sang Foo Fighters' "My Hero" with a surprisingly deep voice that caressed her skin like high-quality suede. As he trailed off, he leaned down and brushed his lips across hers. It should have been suave, but he flinched when he touched her and his hands were shaking, which made it adorable instead. "What do you think?"

"Wow." Candy swallowed so her voice would quit squeaking. "Jody works in the salon upstairs. Why don't you go take that stuff off and I'll see what I can do as far as tailoring your shirt and drop it off on my break." Which meant the last twenty minutes until her break were going to be spent pulling the thread out of the seams without breaking it so she could use it to stitch this shirt by hand and hoping no other customers showed up. This burnout had a lot more to him than miles of flannel and half destroyed oversized jeans. His little hesitation when he touched her sold it. He had some confidence, but not too much. How could a girl not go for that?

He tightened his grip on her arms. His hands were sweaty, but hers were too at this point. "You'd do that for me?"

"You're taking me out to dinner when you get into this band. Don't forget."

He leaned in again. "You gonna dress me all the time?"

"You bet." She rose up on her toes to close the distance he was hesitating over. "Go on. The sooner I get my hands on this shirt, the sooner I'll be done." Measurement. Damn, if she didn't know how much to take it in he was either going to be swimming or cased like a sausage. She measured the extra fabric with her fingers. Oh gawd, his name. She didn't even know his name yet. "Hey, what's your name?"

"Tyler." He leaned in for another kiss but changed direction to her cheek and tried to cover it by giving her arms a squeeze. Another thing she needed to work on with him, confidence. If he was going to front the hottest band in the area, he needed to have the confidence to charm Satan into doing good deeds.

He had the clothes back out in a few minutes, paid, and headed for the salon. After he left, Candy leaned against the desk. Lots of guys hit on her here. Some of them she'd even dated. She'd never let one kiss her though. Technically, she wasn't supposed to have let him use his mother's credit card, but if he was going to steal a credit card, he'd have gone for Master Card, Mr. Visa or Ms. Discover, not a department store card that confined him to a place mainly catering to up and coming professionals, soccer moms, and blue-haired old ladies.

Candy shook herself. She had a little more than an hour between now and the end of her break to take in the seams on this shirt and deliver it. With more time and a sewing machine, she'd have deconstructed the whole thing, but she'd never figured out how to fit her sewing machine into her purse. If she had, she could have made a lot more money and a lot more sales for the store, tailoring between customers.

The phone rang. "Who do you think I am, Doug Henning?"

"Jody, if anybody can make him look good, it's you." Candy picked the first side seam out and smoothed the fabric out on the desk. If she could take it in enough at the waist, the stripes would make it look like he had shoulders. A gym. The boy needed a gym desperately.

"Then nobody can make this dork look good."

"Trust me. All he needs is the visual and that dork will be a swan."

"To get a swan you have to start with some kind of bird. You sent me a daddy longleg spider."

Daddy longleg spider? He didn't look like a spider. Tyler was adorable and sweet and pretty damn charming already. With a little work, well, Jon Bon Jovi had better start thinking about his pension. "Ask him to sing for you."

"I'm going to have to take two inches off to get rid of the split ends. I think he's been washing his hair with bar soap."

"Ask him to sing." Candy searched the desk. Somebody must have thrown out the pins she was hoarding. Paper clips would have to do.

"Fine. I'll see what I can do, but Gina's freaking out. His skin looks like he's been beaten with a bag of nickels. A dirty bag."

Ouch. No fair. They better not be saying this stuff in front of him. It wouldn't do anything for his confidence. "So you can start by washing his face. I'll be up there in a little while with his clothes. I have to do a little alteration for him."

"Fine. He's out of wash anyway. See ya."

Candy hung up the phone and went to work on the shirt.

"Hi there. I didn't know you did alterations here."

Candy glanced up. Middle aged Romeo starting to gray. He'd be good for at least a hundred bucks. "Well, only for very special customers. Can I help you find something?" She arched a little to show off the assets without pausing in her tailoring.

"Maybe you can. Unless you're busy."

"I can multitask."

"Okay. I need a couple of new shirts for work. My wardrobe is looking stagnant and the clients are starting to drift."

"Really? What do you do?" Candy tucked her needle away. She had time. Even if she had to skip dinner, she could have one shirt done by the time Jody was finished.

"Advertising and public relations."

"So you need something fresh." She walked around the desk editing her original assessment of his potential. If he needed a new look for work, she might get him for a couple hundred, which would secure her lead over that bitch in juniors. "Let's see what we can do."

Forty-three minutes later, Candy skidded through the doors of the salon. Tyler sat in a chair with highlight foils on his hair, green goo on his face, and a copy of *People* magazine in his hands, chatting with the little old lady next to him.

Jody shuffled over, slouching as though she'd been breaking rocks all day. "*I* am a miracle worker. Next time you want me to rescue somebody, give me six months' lead time so I can trim and style over time instead of doing damage control."

"I'll do my best."

"He's got an amazing voice though. He had the old cow in the chair next to him about in tears because he sang 'Moon River.'"

"Good, good." Candy headed for the chair. "How's it going, Tyler?"

"Great. This is fantastic. I thought I'd be buying a shirt or something today."

"You need to look good for your big audition." The lady next to him patted his hand. "He's going to be famous. I know it. You better hang onto him, young lady."

Candy glanced at Tyler to see how he was taking the optimism, but the facial covered most of his reaction. He rolled his eyes, but that could be anything. "I'm sure he will be. Hey, I got this shirt done for you. Can you try it on under the smock to make sure it fits?"

"I've got a T-shirt on. Is that okay?"

Jody was right, next time they really needed a head start on these emergencies. "Okay, never mind. We'll have to cross our fingers. I was kinda talking while I was finishing it up."

"Who were you talking to?"

"A customer. He's got me tailoring five shirts for him to pick up next week."

"Do you do this for everybody?" Tyler's eyes narrowed under the mask. Already possessive. Good.

"No, but he saw me working on yours and asked if I could do his. Decent money, too." Really decent. The college fund was looking more hopeful all the time.

A timer dinged and Jody pushed her out of the way to poke at Tyler's hair. "Time to rinse. Cross everything that this works."

Gina edged in and touched the facial mask with her fingertips. "Try not to get this wet. It needs to dry completely before we take it off."

"I'll do my best."

Candy checked her watch. Who needed food? "I better get back. Try the shirt on before you go so I can fix it if I have to."

As she hurried out, she took one last look back. Tyler was in the rinse chair with Jody washing the dye out of his hair while trying not to get the facial wet. Hopefully he'd look decent once he got all that stuff off. Jody was good. Still in beauty school at the county Vo Tech, but she had good instincts. Hopefully.

* * * *

Tyler slithered through the kitchen door as quietly as possible. He wished he could burst through the front crowing about how he'd met this great girl and got in the band all in the same day, but Dad was home. Probably should have climbed up the garage drainpipe and in through his bedroom window, but that would have meant not eating again tonight.

His mother walked in while he was rummaging through the fridge.

"How did it go?" she whispered. He stood up and her mouth fell open. "What happened to your hair this time?"

"I got in the band."

"What happened to your hair?"

Tyler touched his hair. It felt less like wire than usual. The girl at the salon had tortured him about using the right stuff when he washed it and conditioning regularly. Have to start using his sister's shampoo. "I met this girl and she thought it would help and it did. I got in the band."

"That's great, honey." Anxiety bracketed her eyes. "Your father isn't going to like it."

"He doesn't like anything I do."

His mother made a noise. "I know."

"Oh my God!" Tiffany shrieked from the doorway.

Tyler and his mother both jumped.

"What's going on?" His father lumbered into the room and the temperature dropped fifteen degrees. He wore a stained undershirt with saggy jeans. "You look like a faggot. What the hell are you wearing?"

Tyler looked down at the shirt. The colors were a little weird, but it fit like skin and made him feel finished in some way he couldn't put his finger on. When he'd shown Candy before he left the store, she'd been very pleased.

"You look like a faggot," Dad repeated, louder this time.

"Roger!" His mother snapped. "Leave him alone. It's very nice. It's good to see him taking an interest in how he looks."

"He looks like a faggot."

Tiffany giggled.

"Shut up, Tiff," Tyler snarled. Should have climbed in the window. Right now he could be lying on his bed, staring at the ceiling and thinking about Candy.

"I think he looks more grown up and professional." His mother set her jaw. "I'm going to give him my credit card so he can go get more clothes like those. Maybe he'll be inspired to go to college."

Her credit card was still in his pocket, but Tyler figured this was a bad time to bring that up.

"He doesn't need to go to college. He needs to grow up and get a job instead of running around looking like—like a homo."

"There's nothing wrong with how he looks and if he wants to go to college, he should. Better than getting stuck in some dead-end job he complains about every night over dinner," his mother shouted.

"What? Like teaching school so he can complain about how much money he's not making for teaching other people's brats?" his father shouted back.

Tyler's stomach contracted to a pinpoint. All they ever did was fight about him. He should chuck it all and go to the Vo Tech to learn something glamorous like engine repair. "Stop it! I hate you people. I hate this house!" Tyler stomped upstairs and slammed his bedroom door. His room was always clean, clothes put away, desk and dresser cleared, bed made. Never knew when Dad was going to pull a surprise inspection and confiscate anything he thought was out of place.

Throwing himself on his bed, still dressing in the clothes Candy picked out for him, Tyler stared at the Rage Against the Machine poster on the wall. The whole day had been awesome until he got home. When he'd told Mom about the audition this morning on the way to school, she'd insisted he get some new clothes. Then he'd met Candy and she'd been so cool. The girls in the salon fussed over him as if he was important and that little old lady gave him ten bucks because he sang "Moon River" for her twice. The guys in the band were impressed with his voice and with the way he looked. They had a paid gig already for Friday and he'd have to rehearse with them every night at their manager's house to get ready.

The band had a manager. He'd never been in a band big enough to have a manager before. And Candy. Man, even if he hadn't gotten in the band, Candy would have made the whole day worth it. So hot and smart. She planned to go to college. Maybe he should think about it too. Even if he ended up being a teacher like his mom, it would be better than driving truck like his dad. Anything would be better than being like his dad.

His mom tapped on his door. Had to be his mom. His dad and Tiff just barged in.

"Yeah?"

"Hi honey." She stepped through the doorway and scanned the room. "I wanted you to know I'm proud of you for trying this. You've worked very hard and even if it doesn't pan out, you'll know you did your best."

"Thanks, Mom."

She swallowed. "And I do want to you go back to the store and get some more clothes like these. You look very nice. Even your hair." She smiled a little. "It is shorter."

"Yeah."

She sat on the end of the bed and folded her hands in her lap. "So you met a girl. What's she like?"

Tyler shrugged. "She's pretty. She works at the store and she helped me pick this stuff out."

"What's her name?"

"Candy." He wanted to say, *no Mom, I'm not gay*, but that would be rude.

His mother nodded, her expression relaxing. "Well, I hope she's there tomorrow so she can help you pick out some more clothes like these. Try to keep it under two hundred dollars."

Two hundred bucks? His mother must be really relieved. "Thanks, Mom."

"Of course." She patted his foot.

"Hey, Mom," he said as she stood to leave. "I told Candy I'd take her out to dinner if I got in the band."

"What do you need? Money, the car, or both?"

"Both?" He grinned. If she was feeling generous, he should take advantage. Candy would be a lot more impressed if he took her out in a car instead of riding the city bus.

She sighed smiling. "When?"

"I'll ask her tomorrow." Tyler couldn't stop the grin spreading up from his chest and across his face. It was as if the fight with his dad never happened. He'd gotten in the band and was going to see Candy again tomorrow. All was right with the world.

* * * *

When he walked into the young men's section the next day after school, she was standing at the counter sewing and talking to some old guy who looked like he wanted to eat her up. Who wouldn't? She had on this tight green top cut down to there and a tan skirt that showed off her fantastic legs. Tyler's heart stammered. The way she was looking at the guy was exactly the way she'd looked at him yesterday. Like he was special. Important.

All day he'd felt ten feet tall. Everybody at school was psyched about him getting into Touchstone and they were already making plans to come out to McGrudy's for his debut. He'd planned to see if Candy could come too. Then he could introduce her to the band and watch them all pick their tongues up off the floor. But the sight of her with this old guy curdled Tyler's stomach.

He took a step back trying to escape the cloying stickiness of his own stupid fantasy. He should have known a girl like her wasn't going to be alone. That guy was probably one of her many sugar daddies. How many of them did she kiss? He licked his lips trying to remember how she tasted, but could only taste the stale coffee he'd gotten at school while he was waiting for the bus to bring him here. Mom was going to be disappointed if he didn't come home with some new stuff though. He'd have to suck it up.

Candy glanced up from her sewing when he stopped by the desk. Her smile lit up. "Tyler! How did it go?" She dropped the shirt in her hand and reached for him. The guy at the desk scowled as he followed her movements. "Did you get in?"

"Yeah." He forced a smile. That coffee was burning a hole in his stomach.

"That's fantastic." She threw her arms around his neck. "I'm so excited. When are you taking me to dinner? I expect to be paid for my services, y'know."

Tyler put his arms around her waist. Jeez, he was getting hard. "I was going to ask you if you were free tomorrow, but you looked busy." He pulled away hoping she hadn't noticed his boner.

"Busy? Oh, this is another customer of mine."

Another customer. Nice.

The old guy had held out his hand. "Joe Goldman. Didn't mean to move in on your territory."

Tyler shook his hand. Was this guy shitting him? Move in on his territory? As if Tyler had any hope of competing against a guy like this.

"Joe saw me working on your shirt yesterday and asked if I'd do some tailoring for him too. Then he decided to come in today to see if I'd skipped school so I could do it, even though I told him it would take a week." She shot Joe a mock dirty look.

"I didn't think you'd skip school. I thought you might have stayed up all night. If you want to get ahead in this world, you have to go that extra mile."

They sounded so easy together. Like they'd known each other a long time. Joe's clothes fit good. He stood straight but not like there was a steel rod down his spine. Confident, like a real man. The kind of man girls like Candy wanted to be with. Tyler tried to copy the pose, but his shoulders wanted to climb up his neck, so he eased back into his familiar slouch. The guy was watching him as if he could read his mind. Bastard.

"For me, that extra mile means sleeping at night so I can get good grades and doing your tailoring on my day off."

"Unless you're going out with him." Joe Goldman nodded toward Tyler.

Candy turned to Tyler with that bright smile lighting her face again. "I do have the night off tomorrow."

Dinner and the gig on Friday would have been great, but if he didn't get her tomorrow, she might end up going out with this guy. "Great. I've got rehearsal at seven, but I can get you about five at your place and then you could come to rehearsal with me."

"That would be awesome."

Joe sighed. "My shirts will never be done."

Candy sneered at him. "Don't you worry about your shirts. I meet my commitments."

"I'm gonna play my first gig with the band on Friday. Can you come?" Tyler asked before they got too cozy again. The band was the only thing he had going for him over the old guy.

"Friday? Already? I work Friday, though." She huffed. "Man. I wanna go."

"The store closes at nine-thirty." Joe checked his watch even though it wasn't either Friday or anywhere near closing. "Where is your band playing?"

Tyler paused for a minute to savor the words. *Where is your band playing?* His band. "McGrudy's. It's out on State Road."

Candy made a small noise in her throat. "It's way out there. I'll have to see. But tomorrow for sure. Come on and I'll write down my phone number and address for you."

"My mom really likes your taste in clothes. She said I could get a couple more things."

"Fantastic." Candy bent over behind the desk. Tyler glanced away before he started staring and caught Joe admiring her ass. Maybe it wasn't such a horrible thing to do. "We need to get you into something for your show Friday, too. Joe, you're getting bumped for an emergency order."

"I thought you met your commitments."

"I am giving you ample warning. It's going to get done, but it's going to take a little longer than expected."

"I knew it. I'm going to have to hire you to work in my office so I can get you to do my tailoring for me."

Candy laughed as she handed Tyler a piece of paper with her phone number and address.

Chapter 2

Candy paced around her room with the portable phone stuck to her ear. "He asked me to go see the band play Friday, but I have to work." Being home in the afternoon was weird. Between her job and school, she didn't have to spend much time here. Not really a bad thing, but a thing nonetheless.

"So? Call in sick," Jody said.

"I'm not calling in sick." Candy checked her look. Tight dark wash jeans. Filmy black shirt. Leopard print heels. Perfect hair and makeup. Dangling earrings. Slick and complete. And Joe's shirts were finished and folded in a bag by the door so he could pick them up at the store tomorrow and pay her.

"Why not?"

"Because I'm not sick."

"You're going to make me leave the club between sets to come get you."

"Would you?" Of course she would. Jody wanted to get backstage and get her hands on Jason Callisto. It was all she'd been able to talk about for months and that was before she had a valid opening.

"If I have to, but you have to promise to introduce me to the band."

Bingo. "I'm going to meet them tonight. I'm sure it'll be fine." The doorbell rang. "That's him. I gotta go."

"You are so lucky."

Candy walked through her empty house. "Yeah. Lucky. See you tomorrow." She set the phone on the charger on the table under the last family photo from seven years ago. Mom, Dad, and precious Candace. Six months after the picture was hung, Mom ran off, Dad started working all the time and, as soon as she could, so did Candy. "Hi, Tyler. Ready to go?"

"If you are. Shouldn't I say hello to your parents or something?" He was dressed in the green button-down shirt and straight leg jeans she'd picked for him, and even a couple of days on the skin and hair care regimen made a difference. Between her and Jody, they were going to make a rock star out of him if it killed them.

"Nobody home." She snatched her purse off the table before she closed the door behind her. "Where are we going to dinner?"

"Mama Lena's?"

Next up on the hit list was his lack of confidence. Mama Lena's was always good. The sit-down restaurant impressed her because half the time her dates thought McDonald's bought them a park hopper pass to her body. "I love Mama Lena's."

He also had a car. A dark blue Grand Marquis with bumper stickers that read "My Child Made Honor Roll at Fort Island Elementary" and "My Child Made Honor Roll at South High School." Pretty nice part of town. No wonder his mom could hand him a credit card to go shopping. After they ate, he drove her to a residential neighborhood not far from the restaurant. A beat-up car sat in the driveway and the living room lights were on.

"You'll like the guys. They're all really nice." Tyler hurried her up the path. Before he knocked, he smiled at her. "You look really pretty tonight."

"Thanks. You look great, too."

"Thanks to you."

"You fill the clothes out good." She grinned. He did. All through dinner she'd been wishing he'd sat on the same side of the booth as her so she could at least feel his thigh against hers. Wouldn't have happened. Every time she'd brushed his leg under the table, he'd moved it as if he thought he was crowding her.

He knocked.

A stocky, middle-aged man with a buzz cut answered. "Hello Tyler. You brought a guest."

"This is my girlfriend, Candy." Tyler settled his arm around her shoulders as if she might crumble if he pressed too hard.

Girlfriend? That was fast. Maybe he had more confidence than she'd thought. Candy held out her hand. "Hello, it's nice to meet you."

The older man softened as he shook her hand. "And it's nice to meet you too, Candy. I'm Mr. Dale, the boys' manager."

Touchstone had a manager? Most of these garage bands were lucky if they had one member with his shit together enough to book gigs. But then Touchstone was doing better than most garage bands.

"Come on inside. Jeff and Michael are downstairs. Brian and Jason are running late as usual. Candy, would you like something to drink?"

"No, thank you."

Tyler took her hand and led her to a basement door. Downstairs were two more long-limbed rejects from the flannel parade.

"You brought a fucking girl?" the one with the bass shouted.

"Jeffery!" Mr. Dale barked. "Watch your language."

"But it's practice, not the school dance."

"I—I didn't—" Tyler stammered.

"It's not a problem." Mr. Dale put up his hands. "You boys should perform in front of any audience you can get. Michael, clear the recycling off the couch so Candy can sit down."

The kid behind the drums shuffled to the bowed flowered couch along the wall and started moving bundles of newspapers off it. The doorbell rang and Mr. Dale went to answer it.

"I'm Bear," he said when she leaned down to help. "Only my parents and Mr. Dale call me Michael."

"Candy."

"You're really pretty."

"Thank you."

"You and Tyler serious?"

Candy glanced at Tyler. He was fiddling with a microphone, but his attention was on her. "Yeah." As serious as a first date got anyway. None of these schmoes could probably manage a girlfriend and a bourgeoning music career so it would give Tyler some points in their eyes.

"Figures. Mr. Dale ask you if you wanted something to drink? He probably did, huh?"

"He did, but thanks. Pretend I'm not here." Candy sat down and tried to be invisible.

Tyler was talking to Jeff. Michael went back to messing with his drums. Two more boys thundered down followed by the heavier tread of Mr. Dale. The dark-haired one stopped when he hit the bottom. "Who brought a date? Bear!"

Bear held up his hands. "It wasn't me."

"I'm sorry." Tyler glanced around the room. "I didn't know it was a problem."

"It isn't." Mr. Dale clasped the dark haired boy's shoulder. "Say hello to Candy, Jason."

"We can't have somebody here watching us practice. He just started and he still sucks with us." The boy gestured toward Tyler who was turning an awful shade of red that clashed with his hunter green shirt.

"Then it's a perfect time for him to get used to playing with the band and you all need to practice together in front of an audience. Say hello." Mr. Dale angled Jason toward her.

The blond, who dressed as if he was still mourning the death of hair metal, stepped around them and approached her with his hand out. "Hi, I'm Brian."

She stood to shake his hand. "Hi. I think you shop at my store. I work in young men's."

"Uh, yeah." Brian scuffed the floor with the toe of his sneaker. "With my mom."

Candy remembered him now, and he didn't dress like this when he was with his mother. This must be his rock-star look, heaven help him.

"I'm Jason." Jason hadn't made it as far as a flannel, but his jeans and T-shirt had seen better days. "It's not going to be perfect, you know."

Hopefully they didn't go onstage dressed like this because with the exception of Tyler they looked as if they shopped in the Goodwill dumpster. Jody had never said anything about what a visual mess they were. "What?"

"We're practicing. It's not going to be perfect." Jason clenched his fists. Brian elbowed him.

"What? It's not. He just started." Jason angled his thumb at Tyler, who still clashed with his shirt.

"I don't expect it to be perfect. That's why it's called practice." Candy smiled. Sounded pretty good. Mr. Dale was smiling too, so it must have been. Jason didn't look any happier, but he did walk away.

Mr. Dale sat down on the couch with her. "So what do you think?"

"I haven't heard them."

"You've never seen them play?" He frowned.

"I work a lot and I have school."

He nodded. "And what are your grades like?"

"A's and B's in AP and honors classes."

He nodded again. "Your parents must be proud."

Candy made a noncommittal noise because it seemed as if she should respond. Her father hadn't seen a report card in five years. The school didn't even have his signature on file. She'd forged his name so if they did compare it would be the same.

"How long have you and Tyler been dating?"

"This is our first date."

Mr. Dale was starting to look like a bobble head dog. "Tell me, what do you think makes a band successful?"

"I don't know. Good songs?" Candy clasped her hands in her lap and hoped Mr. Dale would go away. When older guys talked to her this much at the store they were usually hitting on her and all she had to do was let them know she was underage and they lost interest, but Mr. Dale already knew she was underage. She was dating the singer in the band he managed. Or was he a pervy old man?

"That's part of it, but do you really think it was songs alone that got the Beatles where they were?"

"I don't know." The Beatles? How old was this guy?

"I don't think it is. I think a lot of it had to do with the way they looked. Four handsome, well-dressed boys. They had half the battle won before the first note."

"The Rolling Stones were uniformly ugly and they were just as big."

He grinned as if his star student had hit the nail on the head. "I think they had something else going for them that you're too young to understand."

Okay, how old did he think *she* was? Twelve? "I'm sorry, but Mick Jagger has the sex appeal of a broken suitcase and I don't want to get into the others."

Mr. Dale laughed loud enough that the boys stopped what they were doing. He clapped her on the shoulder. "You are a very clever girl. Now look at my boys and tell me what you see."

Candy studied the band. They had gone back to their discussion and for a minute, all she saw was Tyler. He stood out. The sloppy jeans, ragged T-shirts and flannels the others were all wearing accented how good Tyler looked. Brian looked as if he'd made an attempt with his hair, but he only succeeded in looking like an over-processed David Coverdale. Every one of them had skin problems that could have been solved with the routine application of soap and water and the occasional moisturizer.

But Tyler. Oh, Tyler looked good. He wasn't any taller than the others, but with his shoulders squared he appeared to have a couple of inches on all of them. He had a brightness about him that came from looking good and knowing it. Candy smiled. He looked like the kind of boyfriend who would have all the girls in her school swooning.

"I know. He stands out like a peacock." Mr. Dale nodded, smiling. "I almost didn't recognize him when he showed up to audition. We'd seen him before, of course, but when he arrived the other night, he was a different boy. He looked like a lead singer. He said you did it." Mr. Dale leaned back on the arm couch.

"Thanks."

"You did an excellent job. What I need to know is, can you do it for the rest of them?"

Candy's mouth fell open. He wanted her to make them over? All of them? This was turning into a much bigger project than she'd planned on while watching Tyler wander around her section of the store the other day.

"These boys could be big. I know they could. They have a very good sound and they have drive. In this era of MTV, we need a good image, too. Once we have those pieces in place, we'll start pursuing a record contract and a top-notch producer. And while the boys are working on their record, we'll be looking at video scripts for the first single. I can handle the business side of things, but I don't know the visual side. You do. We need your help."

Record contract? Producer? Video scripts? There were scripts for music videos?

"Well?"

The band started playing and volume alone could have been the reason she didn't answer. Mr. Dale would think that anyway. Make over a band, like a professional stylist. That would look good on college and scholarship applications. As much as Jeff and Jason had bitched about this just being practice, they sounded tight. Tyler could have been singing with them for months instead of a couple of days. Touchstone could be the first line on her professional resume. "This isn't going to be free," she said between songs. "Clothes cost money."

"I've been holding the money they earn from their gigs for reinvestment and I have a bit of my own to invest."

"My friend Jody can do their haircuts. If we don't do it in the salon, she can do it for free. She's just a student, but she's good. She did Tyler's hair and she always does mine. And her friend Gina will probably pitch in with the skin care." Candy bit her lip. "I could probably cut costs on clothing if I went through the thrift stores and got creative."

"Now she's thinking." Mr. Dale smiled.

Candy looked over the band again, guessing their sizes. All of them except Bear were far too scrawny. If she kept herself to a couple colors, it would help make them look like a group instead of a bunch of guys who happened to climb on stage at the same time. The trick would be not making them look like bridesmaids. This was going to require hours of hunting through thrift stores and more hours on the bus getting from one to the other. Between work, school, and tailoring there weren't going to be enough hours in the day for a while. "When is this all going to be due?"

"We have a little time. I don't want to be looking for a record contract until next year. The boys are too young yet and I don't want to put them under that kind of pressure until they're at least out of high school. Putting them on the road to tour before they're old enough to drink would be cruel."

Gosh, yes, because heaven knows as famous rock stars nobody would serve them if they were underage. How could Mr. Dale be so smart and so dumb at the same time? "One more thing."

"What's that?"

"They need to work out. All of them. Heroin thin is out."

Mr. Dale held out his hand and it took her a minute to realize he wanted her to shake it. He was treating her as an adult. "We have a deal. I think I'm going to enjoy working with you."

"You know I'm only sixteen."

"I am aware, but you seem to be a young lady of extraordinary maturity."

* * * *

Candy glanced across the dressing room at the sound of Jody and Jason bickering. Well, Jody was bickering. Jason was looking at her as if he couldn't figure out why she was there. Jason's sister Connie was consumed with reaming out Jeff for spilling a Coke on his pants. Nothing unusual, so Candy went back to the repair she had to finish before the next set. Tyler sat down next to her and kissed her cheek.

"How's it going?"

"Be going better if Bear would stop splitting his pants."

"Why won't he wear the stretchy ones?"

"Because he wants his ass to be a pain in my ass." Candy tied off the last stitch and snipped the thread with the tiny scissors she wore on a yellow ribbon around her neck. Mr. Dale had given them to her because he didn't want her to have to carry around a pair of real scissors in a crowded club.

Tyler cupped her cheek turning her gaze to him. "Don't run off."

"I was going to give Bear his pants."

"Let him come get them himself." Tyler leaned down and kissed her. As always, he was soft and sweet. Candy closed her eyes, shutting out the noise in the room. Her body warmed, aching to be alone with him. His fingers tangled through her hair, sending shivers down her back. She moaned, parting her lips.

"You done with my pants?" Bear demanded, yanking her back to the present.

Tyler leaned back, groaning.

Bear stood in front of them wearing only his tighty-whities with his fists on his hips.

Candy threw the pants at him before turning back to Tyler. Before they could connect, a bouncer was standing at the door bellowing that the band had five minutes to get their asses on stage or they weren't going to get paid. Tyler gave her another peck on the cheek before he left.

Candy busied herself cleaning up her things. Connie waved at her on the way out the door. After tucking away the rest of her stuff so she'd just have to grab her plastic sewing caddy when they left, Candy went out too.

The boys were already on stage and no way she was getting anywhere near it. People had started staking out spots up front lately. Most of them female. That meant she was doing her job well. Where the girls were, the boys would follow. And according to Mr. Dale, that equaled popularity across the board. It also meant every gig she missed for work she sweated out thinking he'd find somebody else.

She headed for the bar. One of the things Mr. Dale negotiated was unlimited drinks for the band and their crew. Since they were all underage, the bar didn't mind. Pop was cheap and easy to serve, and nobody got too drunk to perform on Pepsi. On her way to the low wall leading down to the tables between the bar and the stage, she spotted a man leaning against the bar watching her. He lifted his drink to her so she changed direction.

"Hello, Joe. What are you doing here?"

"Checking out your boy." He waved his drink toward the stage. "They're pretty good."

"I told you they were."

"I have to see these things for myself." He turned to face her. "Valley Mall is having a big celebration this summer. All summer long they're having bands on the weekends to draw people in to shop."

The bartender set a plastic cup of Pepsi on the bar beside her. She smiled at him in thanks. "And?"

"I have ten slots to fill. The kind of crowd your boys draw, I could see them taking up three or four."

"What does it pay?"

He grinned. "That's why I like you. You don't go all squeally at the thought of a gig. You want to know what the pay is first. I planned to pay the bands a hundred."

"Touchstone's going rate is two hundred." Not entirely true. They got two hundred here, but most places paid a hundred. Mr. Dale had been coaching her on the art of negotiation.

He nodded. "I may be able to see my way clear to pay one-fifty. The shows are in the afternoon, so it wouldn't interfere with their evening shows and it would expose them to a wider audience."

"Moms and kids who aren't old enough to get into the underage clubs?"

Joe shrugged. "You have me there. What if we threw in all the free pop you could drink?"

"They can drink a lot of pop." Candy licked her lips. A wider audience that wouldn't interfere with evening gigs would be good. The extra money would cover equipment and transportation, and replace the pants Bear kept splitting. "I'll put you in touch with the band's manager, Alexander Dale."

"How about a job?"

Candy had been raising her cup to her lips, but she hesitated. "A job? For who?"

"You."

Candy put her drink down before she dropped it. A job? How many shirts did he need altered? "What are you talking about?"

"I've got an internship open in my office. Pays more than your little shop-girl job in less hours, and you'd have nights and weekends free to follow your band around. Of course, I'd be your boss so you'd actually have to listen to me when I tell you to do something and the pace is more demanding. You won't have time to sew on the job anymore."

Unreal. Joe had only known her a couple of months. He'd bought almost a complete wardrobe from her and had every piece tailored. He'd also sent a couple of people to her from his office. Thanks to him, there was no way anyone would beat her out for the sales bonus. But that was because she was a good sales person and a good seamstress. What made him think she'd fit in his marketing firm? "Why?"

"Why what?"

"Why are you offering me this job? There's got to be a college student dying to get it."

"There's a few, but none of them have what you have."

"The ability to sew?"

He studied her face for a long time. "One of them does sew, but none of them have your *je n'est sais quoi*."

"You mean none of them looks as good in a short skirt as I do." She picked up her drink again. The job would be nice. She'd had to miss a lot of Tyler's gigs because of work. It would look really good on her college applications. Too bad she was totally unqualified for it. Either Joe was jerking her chain or he wanted an underage horizontal assistant. No, he'd never shown himself to be the type. When they chatted at the store, he was talking to her about his firm and marketing stuff. He had claimed he wanted the viewpoint of a younger person. Market analysis, he called it.

Joe leaned to look her over. "Not necessarily."

"You remember I'm still underage, right?"

"I've lived with that reality for a while now and if you were working for me I couldn't even flirt with you anymore, but I think having you on staff would make up for it." He shifted his stance against the bar. "I've been watching you build this campaign and it's inspired. For a total amateur, you have a gift for public relations."

Inspired? All she'd done was give the guys a cohesive image so their name was on the lips of every girl in a hundred-mile radius. She'd put together a couple of posters with the help of the art teacher at school and she'd rallied friends to make sure those posters went up in logical high traffic areas. *Did that constitute a marketing campaign?* "But all I did was change the way they looked and put up a few fliers."

"You did more than that." He pointed to the stage. "You put together a look for the band that makes them very identifiable. You gave them a brand. I know they're a bunch of high school kids and they look like pros. And not just that. I've heard people talking about them. Not only kids, adults."

"I didn't do that."

"You designed the posters advertising their gigs. You got them hung up in a timely fashion at the right places. You've written up the press releases that get them talked about." He poked her shoulder. "You have made the right connections to get them even more good press. Everybody knows where Touchstone is playing on any given weekend even if they don't frequent these kinds of clubs."

Press releases. She'd forgotten about those. "You told me to write press releases. You had to teach me how."

"I suggested it, but that doesn't mean you'd actually do it. You've got drive. Come work for me and we can point your drive in a useful direction instead of leaving it to sell shirts at the mall."

Candy chewed her lips. Once or twice, she'd asked Joe questions instead of just listening to what he told her about marketing. That's how she figured out how to do most of what she'd done for the band. It seemed like the natural thing to do. If she was working for him, she'd see him more often to ask more questions. "Will you help me work on a bigger, better campaign for the band?"

He shook his head, chuckling. "And you think I'm offering you this job because you're cute. Of course we'll work on a bigger campaign for the band. What do you say?"

"Are you kidding? Yeah. When do I start?"

"Why don't we wait until school's out? You have to give notice at your job."

Candy threw her arms around his neck. "This is awesome."

"See, now I'm getting the squealing and jumping up and down."

Candy pushed away from him. "Oh shut up."

"Is that any way to talk to your new boss?"

"Was that any way to handle your new employee?"

"I was not handling. I was hugging."

She shoved his shoulder. "Whatever. I gotta go tell my boyfriend the news."

"I think he's busy."

"I know where to wait until he's available." Candy grabbed her Pepsi and headed for the side of the stage. Joe didn't blow smoke. If he said working for him would be better money than at the store, it would be. Even the same money for less time would be fantastic. Office hours. She wouldn't have to miss anymore of Tyler's gigs, which meant she could keep all those other girls away from him. And if Joe was going to help her build a real campaign it would be good for the band. A real professional campaign would get them known outside her hundred-mile radius and make it a lot easier for Mr. Dale to get them a record contract.

The last set wound down, or rather up, as planned and the lights went out. The crowd went nuts, screaming for more. Tyler grabbed her as he came off stage. "How were we?"

"Awesome." She wrapped her arms around him. He was sweaty and hot. "Guess what?"

"What?"

"Joe offered me a job in his office."

"Joe who?"

"Joe Goldman. From the ad agency. He's got a gig for you guys too."

Jason grabbed his arm. "Come on. Encore."

Tyler jerked away from Jason. "Fuck off, man. I'm busy."

"Yeah, busy playing a gig." Jason grabbed for him again.

This time Tyler took a swing at him, but Jason ducked.

"You need to get your ass back on stage or you are so done," Jason shouted.

"Hey, cut it out." Brian stepped between them. "Come on, Tyler. It's three songs and then you can suck face with Candy all you want."

Tyler didn't look at him. His gaze was firmly fixed on Candy's. "Don't take it."

"Are you nuts? It's a real job. He's going to help me build a real campaign for you guys. He can make you really famous."

"I don't want you working for him."

"Real campaign?" Jason crowded Brian into them. "Like real advertising?"

"Yes. Yes, he said it would be my special project."

"He just wants to fuck you." Tyler clenched his fists.

Candy folded her arms. "Well, he's going about it all wrong. If I'm working for him, he can't do anything inappropriate or I can sue, and he knows I'm underage anyway. You need to finish the show."

"Candy." He reached for her again, but let his hands drop. "I love you."

Chapter 3

All sound in the room stopped. All the people, the rest of the band, everyone, disappeared. "You love me?"

"Yeah, baby, I love you and I'm asking you to do this for me." This time when he reached for her, he made contact. She let him pull her close. "I love you and I don't want you working for this old man who's gonna mess with your head and steal you away from me."

He loved her. Nobody had ever said they loved her before, unless she counted her Mom. But she really wanted this job, and it would be good for them, too. She needed time to explain. The crowd was giving up on the encore. If they didn't go out, word would get around and people might stop showing up. "You need to do your encore."

"Don't you love me?"

"Yes, I love you." She brushed her fingers through his sweaty hair. He was so sweet. Nothing was too much to do for her. Every day she worked, he rode the bus out to the mall before rehearsal so he could have dinner with her during her break. The days she didn't work, they were together before band practice. He brought little presents and serenaded her. One day he'd jumped on the edge of the fountain and sang Tonic's "If You Could Only See" to her. "I do love you," she whispered. He'd never hear it over the noise, but it didn't matter. "Go do your encore."

He kissed her hard and ran out on stage.

Candy weaved.

"Everything okay?" Connie asked.

"I'm not sure."

"Come on, let's go backstage." Connie pulled her into the deserted dressing room. Another woman followed them. She looked enough like

Jason and Connie that Candy was willing to bet she was yet another sister. "What's going on?"

"I got offered a dream job and Tyler doesn't want me to take it."

"Why?" Connie settled her on the couch and the other sister sat on her opposite side, hemming her in.

"He doesn't like Joe. I think he's jealous."

"You're not going to let some guy run your life, are you?" the other sister asked.

"Tessa!"

"Well, she isn't, is she?" the other sister, apparently Tessa, shot back.

"I don't know what to do." Candy clenched her fists in her lap. To further his career and her own, she had to take the job, but if she took the job, he might break up with her. Then he'd be famous and she'd be without him. Tyler would have what he wanted. She'd have a great job, which six months ago would have thrilled her, but she wouldn't have him. What did she want more? The job and for Tyler to become famous? Or to have Tyler and gamble that she and Mr. Dale could do a good enough job on their own?

Tessa started to kneel on the floor, took a good look at it and dragged a folding chair over so she could sit in front of Candy. "How do you know this other guy?"

"He shops at the store where I work, and I've done some alterations for him."

"Is he cute?" Connie put her arm around Candy's shoulders.

"Connie!" Tessa leaned over her knees. "Tell us a little about this guy and this job he's offering you."

"He's old enough to be my dad."

"So? Is he cute?"

"I don't know. I'm not interested in him. I love Tyler." *And he loves me. He said he did. Right in front of everybody.*

"Connie, it doesn't matter if this guy is cute. He's offering her a job. A good one." Tessa glanced at Candy. "It is a good one, right?"

"It's a dream job."

"But do you trust him?" Tessa took her hands. Candy felt like the flag in tug-of-war.

"Tyler or Joe?"

"The guy with the job."

"Sure. He owns the Goldman Group."

"Joseph Goldman?" Tessa's fingers clenched around Candy's.

"Who's Joseph Goldman?"

"Indiana's most eligible bachelor. He's worth a couple million dollars and he's not old enough to be your dad. Your sugar daddy, maybe."

"He's worth a couple million and he shops at the mall?" Connie sneered.

"How do you think he got to be worth a couple million? He watches where his money goes. Besides, if I was running a PR firm, I'd hang out at the mall too. What better place to find out what people were talking about? What's the job?"

"It's an internship in his office."

"The local one?"

"What other one is there?" Joe was a millionaire? He didn't act like one. Not that Candy had a lot to compare him to. He stopped at the store every other week or so. If he bought anything anywhere in the store, he carried it to her register so she could have the sale. The only jewelry he wore was a watch that didn't look too special. Was there another Joe Goldman? Or another Goldman Group?

"He's got offices in New York and Los Angeles."

"But he's been helping me with stuff for the band."

"Really?" Tessa and Connie exchanged a look. What was so fucking special about Joe helping her with the fliers? He made some layout and wording suggestions. So did the art teacher. Candy did the hard part by herself. "So you'd be able to pick his brain about more advertising for Jason's band."

"Sure. He said they could be my special project."

Connie grabbed her hands. "You have to take this job."

"But what about Tyler? He said he loves me."

Connie's expression melted toward a heartfelt aw, but Tessa spoke first. "You need to make him understand. This is going to be good for his music career. No, this is going to be *great* for his music career. You'll have access to somebody with a lot of money and a lot of know-how to get them noticed. Convince him. And if that doesn't work, fuck him."

"I'm not going to dump him to help him."

Tessa shook her head. "I didn't mean dump him, I meant fuck him. Literally. Men can't think with both heads at the same time. If you've got him thinking with the one between his legs, he won't protest with the one on his shoulders."

Connie didn't argue. This must be what it was like to have older sisters.

The backstage door burst open and the guys tumbled in, still high from the great show. Tyler yanked Candy from between Tessa and Connie and swung her around, kissing her. He only let her go to change so he could help tear down the stage. Candy gathered their stage clothes from where they were dropped. If she threw one load in tonight before bed, she'd have time to get everything washed for tomorrow's gig, depending on what time she got dropped off.

In the usual after-show chaos, she didn't have much time to do more than give Tyler a kiss before hitching a ride home with Tessa, Connie, and Jason so she should have been expecting the doorbell the next morning. Tyler stood outside, soaked from walking to her house from the bus stop in the frigid downpour that had started about dawn and showed no signs of letting up. "Hi, baby."

"You must be freezing." She peeled his jacket from his shoulders, but he wrapped his arms around her before she got it off.

"Not anymore." He buried his face in her hair. "Your dad home?"

"No."

"Good." He slid his hands under her shirt. His fingers were icy and she flinched.

"You really need to warm up first."

"I thought you'd warm me up."

She pulled away laughing. "I happen to have some of your clothes here for you to change into. Black jeans and a black shirt. You're gonna look like Johnny Cash, but the colors are still in the dryer." The basket of still-warm clothes sat next to the couch. She pulled out his things.

"Not a bad thing to look like Johnny Cash." He took the clothes and gave her a kiss before heading to the bathroom to change. "When's your dad coming home?" he called out.

"Don't know. Dad's note said he was going to catch up on some work in the office today. He might be home tomorrow."

"Don't you work tomorrow?"

"Yeah, convenient, huh?" After the argument last week, her father had been scrupulous about not being home when she was. Tyler had believed that the bruise on her shoulder came from a clothing rack.

"Yeah." Tyler walked out grinning.

She didn't point out that she was being sarcastic. Why bother? It was convenient.

Tyler sat down next to her, but instead of easing her onto her back to neck, he took her hands in his. "I meant it yesterday when I said don't want you to take this job."

Shit. She'd been hoping he'd forgotten so she could avoid this confrontation. Tessa's advice about having sex with him floated to the surface of her mind. It wouldn't be a hardship. They hadn't so far, but mostly because they hadn't had the opportunity. Here in the house alone all day, opportunity abounded. "Do we have to talk about this?"

"I just—I don't want you to."

"And what? Stay at the store for the rest of my life?"

"No, you're going to go to college and get a real job."

"I could have a real job now."

Tyler made a face. "He's old."

"Who cares? I want his job not his body."

He closed his fingers around hers. "I love you."

She pulled her hands away. "You keep saying that like it should solve everything. Don't you know what an opportunity this is for both of us?"

"I know it's an opportunity for me to lose you and it's true, I do love you."

"Oh God." Candy walked across the room. "If you really loved me you'd want me to take the job."

"Why?"

"Because—" Candy spun. "Because it's a really good opportunity for both of us."

"And you keep saying *that* like it solves everything." Tyler stood up. The black made him look taller and leaner, older. More mature maybe.

"It does. Do you know who Joe is?"

"Some asshole who's trying to poach my girlfriend."

"No, he's a millionaire. Tessa said he owns a huge public relations firm with offices in New York and Los Angeles."

"Awesome. He's richer than God and just as powerful. Are these supposed to be the selling points?"

"Yes. Do you know what it means for your band? It means I'll have access to the kind of people who do national campaigns. I'll meet people who can really do things for you. I'll know people who actually have money so you can get some good equipment and a truck to haul it around in instead of dividing everything between Jeff's pickup and John's van and hoping it doesn't rain or if it does rain that it doesn't get under the tarp on the truck."

"He's getting a cap." Tyler crammed his hands in his pockets and slouched.

"You could get a real truck. And I'd be able to see you play every time you had a show. Joe said I'd be earning as much money as at the store, but I wouldn't have to work weekends. How can you not see that this is a great thing?"

"Maybe it is a great thing, but I want to be your great thing. I wanna be your hero." Tyler blinked fast.

"That is the most ridiculous thing you've ever said."

"I'm a joke now?"

"No, you're making shit up and clouding the issue."

"What makes you think any of it is going to be true?"

"I've been talking to Joe for months. Why would he lie?"

"Because he wants to fuck you. Why wouldn't he?"

"If I'm working for him he can't touch me. It's against the law. And he knows I'm underage so it's doubly against the law."

"Like that would stop him."

"If I'd known you were going to turn into such an irrational prick, I'd have skipped the job and told him I'd be his mistress."

Tyler stiffened. "Did he ask you to?"

"No. What a stupid question." *Did he really think that about her?* Some of those girls who came to the shows were pretty fast, but he should know she wasn't. Especially not with anyone who wasn't him.

"Now *I'm* stupid?"

"No, you're just—" Candy shook her head. "I'm taking the job whether you like it or not."

"Fine. Have a nice fucking life." Tyler stomped to the door and slammed out.

His jacket was still where she'd hung it to dry on the back of a kitchen chair. A bunch of his clothes were stacked, neatly folded on the chair with more tumbling around the dryer right now. He was going to get all wet. Probably get a sore throat and not be able to sing tonight. Candy threw open the door. Tyler had made it to the end of the driveway, shoulders hunched against the cold. "Tyler, come back."

He ignored her and turned to follow the sidewalk to the bus stop.

"Tyler!" He kept walking away. Just because he was afraid she would leave him for Joe. Of all the stupid things. Tears choked her. He was the first boy to tell her he loved her. The first one she believed really might. "Tyler, please come back!"

He was past the Ferguson's driveway now.

Candy ran into the rain. "Tyler!" she wailed. Mud squelched into her socks as she ran across the yards. "Tyler, please." She grabbed his arm and he finally turned. "Please come back."

"Why? You made up your mind. You're already gone."

"No, I'm not." Candy sobbed. God, she was out here on the street crying like a kid. So humiliating. "I love you and I want to take the job so I can see more of you and help your career. Please, don't make me choose."

"Why? Because you'll choose the job?"

"No, because I won't be able to have either. Please, don't leave me."

He stared at her face. "I don't want to lose you."

"So, you're going to walk away? That doesn't make any sense. Please, can't you trust me? I don't love him. I love you. All the money in the world wouldn't make me leave you."

Tyler stroked her cheek. "You're getting all wet."

Candy's teeth chattered. According to her English teacher, Mrs. Van Wick, April was the cruelest month, but right now, May was kicking its ass.

"Come on. Let's go back inside and get you warmed up." He guided her back to the house. Inside, he held her. Candy clung to him. She still wanted this job. Needed it.

But if he really wanted her not to take it, she'd tell Joe to forget it. It would have to be one more year dividing her time between school, the store, and the band. Then four years of dividing her time between college, the store, and the band. Unless they broke up before then. How bad could it be?

"This is really important to you."

"Forget it." Candy pressed her cheek against his chest. "I'll work it out somehow."

"It's part time? Office hours?" He stroked her hair.

"Just forget about it. I'll tell Joe no."

"Do you really love me?" he whispered against her temple.

"Yes, I really love you." Her chest burned with it. She dug her fingers into his back. All she could smell was laundry softener. In the basement, the dryer buzzed.

"If you want to work for Joe, it's okay with me."

"Really?" Her knees buckled.

"You'll be really good at it."

"How do you know?"

He gave a strained chuckle. "Because you're good at everything."

"I'd give it up for you."

"I know. That's why I want you to take it."

Candy stood up on her toes to kiss him. His hands pressed into the small of her back. Her dad wouldn't be home until late, maybe not until after they left for the show. Tyler was hard against her belly. The laundry in the dryer was going to be all wrinkled. Maybe there'd be time to wash it again after. She pulled back a step, stripping off her muddy socks, and taking his hand.

"What?"

"Come with me."

"Where?"

She tugged him toward the hall.

"Candy, where are you taking me?"

He looked genuinely confused, but he went with her.

The hall didn't look any different. Narrow, dim, white walls. Her school pictures hung along one side from kindergarten through fifth grade. Mom took off before the sixth grade photos were sent home. It was all so normal and so new.

"Candy?" He pulled his hand out of hers at the doorway.

"Come on, what are you afraid of?"

"That you're gonna say no at the last minute."

Candy reached into her bedside table and fished out the condoms she'd stolen from her dad's medicine cabinet. "Does it look like I'm going to change my mind?"

* * * *

Tyler parked his car in the driveway. He needed to shower before he went to get Candy at work. If working construction in June sucked, he could only dread August. And January. It was enough to make him really consider college. When Candy came to his graduation party, his mom had been all over her plan to go to college after she graduated next year. Joe had arranged it so next year, she got out of school at lunch to work at his office from then to five, and she got college credit for it because Joe knew people at the university. Over the summer, she was taking some college classes to get a head start. Joe arranged that too.

Fucking Joe walked on water. She tried not to talk about him all the time, but couldn't help herself. Every time his name came up, Tyler wanted to puke. Fucking Joe set the band up with three good gigs at the mall, talked to Mr. Dale about getting them into a recording studio for a demo, and knew the guy who owned the big club by the university that paid half of door for the show, which could be as much as five hundred bucks. Fucking Joe wrecked the afternoons for him without even being around. Usually Tyler picked Candy up at work and took her back to her house so they could have dinner and then sex. Then they'd go to rehearsal and he'd drop her off afterward before heading home. She called it "playing house."

When Tyler walked through the door, his father snarled from his broken down recliner, "What are you doing home?"

A better question was, *What are* you *doing home?* His dad should have been on the road until six. "I just got off work."

"Little fucking freeloader." His dad took a swig from the beer bottle in his hand.

Tyler thought about pointing out that he'd started paying rent as soon as he graduated, but decided against it. From where he stood by the door, he could see Tiff cringing at the top of the stairs. How long had Dad been home and how long had he been drinking? He shifted so that Tiff had a clear path behind him to the front door.

"Nothing to say for yourself?"

"It wouldn't do any good."

"You little shit." His father threw down his beer bottle and heaved himself to his feet. "I want you out of this house."

Tyler clenched his teeth to keep from saying anything. Tiff ran down the stairs and out the door.

"Look what you've done to our family," his father roared. "This is all your fault."

"Where's Mom?" He seemed to remember his mother saying something about a class she was taking this week, but at the time he'd been too busy envying her sitting in an air-conditioned classroom while he humped up and down a ladder all day to pay attention to specifics.

"Not here to protect you." His father took a weaving step toward him.

Tyler did not want to get into a fistfight with his drunken father tonight. Or ever. Tiff was out of the house, so she was safe enough. He didn't know where his mother was to get a warning to her. He lunged out the door, running for his car. Fumbling for the keys, he jumped in, started the car and backed out of the driveway.

"Run, you little shit. And don't stop!" His father stood on the front porch shaking his fist as long as Tyler could see him.

The office Candy worked in was right downtown. He had to circle the block a couple of times to get a parking space. The third time around Candy was standing on the sidewalk watching down the street for him. When she saw his car, her face lit up. She always looked freakishly hot in the conservative skirts and blouses she wore to work with her hair pulled straight back in a barrette. Climbing in the car, she kissed him. "Hi honey, how was your day? No time to shower?"

"The day was fine, but my dad went nuts when I got home so I didn't stick around to shower."

"No problem, you can shower while I'm getting dinner ready." She leaned her head on his shoulder. "I love you. Joe is letting me work on this huge deal. His company is trying to get the California Avocado Growers Association account. He's flying to LA next month to present it. He said he knows somebody who can set him up to meet somebody at Elektra Records. If you have your demo done by then, he could deliver it by hand.

I called Mr. Dale today and told him, so tonight is probably going to be a band meeting."

Great. Perfect end to a perfectly shitty day. Fucking Joe.

* * * *

"You're what?" Jason shouted.

Tyler rubbed his temples. All through dinner, Candy kept talking about that fucking avocado thing and it gave him a headache. Jeff quitting the band wasn't helping.

"Jason, would you please stop yelling?" Mr. Dale rubbed his hands though his short hair.

"Why?" Jason snapped at Mr. Dale before turning on Jeff again. "You stupid, selfish son of a bitch."

"Selfish? *I'm* selfish?" Jeff jabbed himself in the chest with his thumb. "Look, you can pin your whole future on this pipe dream, but I'm not. My mom and dad are willing to pay for school. I'm being a nice guy telling you this far in advance."

"Where are we supposed to find another bass player? Nobody wants to play fucking bass." Jason stomped to the window.

"Look, you've got two months before I go. You can find somebody in that time. You won't have to miss any gigs." Jeff shoved his hands in his pockets. "Mr. Dale, you understand, don't you?"

"Of course I do, son." Mr. Dale steepled his fingers, staring at the tips as if the answers were there. "This is going to delay our demo plans."

"Hey, if you make it big, I can work for you. Do your books?"

Jason banged his head against the wall.

"Boy! Stop that before you dent my wall. Now, who do you know who plays bass and isn't a stoner?"

How late was he going to have to stay out tonight? If his dad was really on a tear, he might stay up. Mom had to come home sometime, but what if they got into it and the fight ran late? He might walk into an even worse situation. Unless he parked down the block and climbed in through the window. That might work. He'd still need to hang out as late as possible with Candy.

But what if Dad got violent with Mom? His father had never done anything like that before, but he'd never been as threatening as he was this afternoon either. Thrown beer bottles were common enough, but today Dad really had looked as if he was coming out swinging. Maybe he should be home early to get in the way if Dad went after Mom or Tiff, though Tiff wasn't stupid. She'd been smart enough to hide upstairs until he'd walked in to create a diversion. She wouldn't go home until she knew it was safe. Her best friend lived three blocks over. Tiff would stay there.

Why was Dad even home so early? He never got home until after Tyler and judging by the number of beer bottles on the table, he'd been at it for a while. Had he lost his job? The guys his dad worked for all seemed to like him and he did his job well. Unless there were cutbacks. If Dad lost his job, what would happen to the house? How would they eat? Mom had a good job, but she didn't earn as much as Dad. Tyler couldn't make up the shortfall. His construction job paid pretty well, but not the kind of money his dad brought down driving truck. What was going to happen to Mom and Tiff?

"Tyler. Tyler!"

Mr. Dale was glaring at him. Everybody else was too, even Jason, making him wonder how long they'd been trying to get his attention. "What?"

"I asked if you knew anybody."

"I know a couple of guitar players, but nobody who's going to want to play bass. Marc Wells is…"

"Marc Wells?" Jason wandered closer to the couch looking as if he'd just been in a near miss with a truck. "You know Marc Wells?"

"I tried out for Soul Torture." Tyler shrugged. At the time he'd been too devastated by not getting into that band to think about anything else. A month later, he'd met Candy and joined this band. "He said I had great range, but I was only seventeen and couldn't get into the places they played. He gave me his number."

Bear shook his head. "He's not going to quit Soul Torture. They're headlining Rockin' On the River this year."

"He wasn't happy last time I talked to him. He said the other guys in his band weren't serious about music anymore."

"Wow, he's got a longer waiting list for students than you do, Jason." Candy's eyes grew round. "He gives clinics up at Guitar Land."

"When was the last time you talked to him?" Mr. Dale asked.

Tyler shrugged. "Three weeks ago at the Agora? He came to see us play."

"Marc Wells came to see us play, and you didn't tell us?" Jeff demanded.

"Like you care," Bear grumbled. "You quit."

"So? That doesn't mean I don't think the band is good."

Tyler scratched the back of his head. At the time he'd been wondering if it would be a good idea to ask Marc to get him a wine cooler for Candy but decided against it. Mr. Dale had a thing about them drinking and he hadn't wanted to get kicked out of the band over it. "I guess it wasn't that important at the time."

"Not important. Jesus." Jason rubbed his face with both hands.

Mr. Dale pointed at Jason. "Watch your language."

"What did Marc say about us? Did he think we were good?" Bear asked.

Tyler frowned. Marc's exact words had been: "at least you have one good guitar player. Most of the pieces are there."

"He thought we were good."

Brian put up both hands. "I would totally switch to bass if we could get Marc Wells."

"No. Why should you have to?" Jason demanded. "It's not fair. It's our band."

"Yeah, it's our band." Brian made a swirling gesture with his finger to take in everyone in the room. "Marc Wells is a way better guitar player than I'll ever be and a way better addition to the band than any bass player we're going to find. If we can get him."

"Why don't you give him a call?" Mr. Dale gestured to the phone. "Ask him if he would like to audition for us."

Candy caught Tyler's arm. "Tell him to keep it quiet. We don't want this to get around until it's a done deal."

"Good thought, Candy," Mr. Dale said. "You must be learning a lot at your job."

Yeah, let's talk about Candy's totally awesome job she's learning so much from working for Fucking Joe. Tyler fished through his wallet until he found the phone number scrawled on a bar napkin. He dialed.

"Yeah?"

"Hi Marc, it's Tyler Franklin from—"

"Touchstone. I remember. How's it going, man?"

"That's what I called to talk about. You said you were thinking about quitting your band." Tyler glanced around the ring of expectant faces. If he could get Marc Wells for the band, maybe he'd be Candy's hero again instead of Fucking Joe.

"What I said was I wasn't happy with my band's lack of direction, but that I didn't have anywhere else to go."

"I might have someplace for you to go." If the others crowded too much closer, they would suffocate him.

"Yeah?"

"Our bass player is quitting."

"I don't play bass. I play guitar."

"Oh totally, I know." Mr. Dale winced and Tyler figured he must have been sounding too much like a kid again. "I mean, I'm aware of that.

We're having a band meeting right now and Brian said he'd be willing to pick up bass if you wanted to join us playing guitar."

"He the dark-haired one?"

"No, Brian's blond."

"Promising." Something clicked at Marc's end of the line, as if he was playing with a lighter or a pen. "I don't know. I don't want to play with a bunch of kids."

"We're not kids. We're all nineteen now. And we've got a manager and a publicist."

"I know." Marc took a deep breath. "I'd have to play with you and see if we work well together. What are you doing tomorrow night?"

Tyler gave them a thumbs up as he gave Marc directions to the house. Candy jabbed him in the side before he hung up. "One more thing. Don't tell anybody."

"Shit, same goes for you. I don't want this getting back to Soul Torture either. What's the address?"

Tyler rattled off Mr. Dale's address before hanging up.

"Is he coming?" Jason had been standing close enough to the phone to hear for himself, but Tyler nodded anyway. Bear and Brian high-fived one another. Candy threw her arms around him and plastered a sloppy wet one on him. At least she wasn't talking about avocados anymore.

"All right you two, that's enough." Mr. Dale tugged Tyler's shoulder. "Good work. Why don't we break early tonight? Give you boys a night off." He shooed them toward the door.

Jeff apologized all the way to the cars, but Candy was already plotting what she was going to put in the press release when Marc officially joined Touchstone.

"Maybe I should call Tracy at *Stage and Scene* and give her a heads-up tomorrow," Candy said as he walked her to the door. He always parked on the street in case her dad came home before he left, but that had never happened before so he wasn't sure why he did it.

"I thought you didn't want anyone to know."

"I don't, but Tracy loves to be on the inside and she might be able to slide it into the Rumor Has It column without naming names so when it does come out we'll already be generating buzz."

"I guess."

Candy unlocked the door. "Are you sure you're okay?"

"Sure. It's just been a weird day."

She stroked his cheek. "I know, but this is going to be for the best in the end, I'm sure of it." Candy wrapped her arms around his neck and kissed him. Her body, so lean and strong, felt so good on his. She was so smart and gorgeous. What was she doing with a loser like him in the first place? His own family didn't want him. "You want to come in and watch a movie or something?" she murmured against his lips.

Or something was promising. It wasn't as if he had anywhere to go anyway. With luck, Dad would fall asleep and he'd be able to climb up the garage drainpipe to his room. But in this mood, Dad wouldn't fall asleep until after midnight and then he might sleep on Tyler's bed trying to catch him climbing in the window. Candy's dad might not even come home tonight. Sometimes he didn't. Then Tyler could sleep on her couch. He wasn't optimistic enough to think he was going to get into her bedroom. "Or something?"

She smiled and pulled him through the door.

Chapter 4

She'd put on a movie anyway, in case her dad came home, and they necked all the way through it the first time. After it rewound they started to watch, but she fell asleep in his arms. Tyler held her, her sleeping weight like an anchor keeping him from getting sucked into a jet turbine. If only he never had to go home and could stay here with her forever. He'd never wanted to be with a girl the way he wanted to be with Candy. His eyes drooped closed despite his best efforts to keep watch for her dad. This was good.

"You little slut!" Candy was jerked out of Tyler's arms, dragging him off the couch with her. "You're as bad as your mother."

Tyler landed on the floor with a jarring thump, echoed by a sharp crack and a wail.

Candy.

He was on the floor and this tall guy had Candy dangling by her shoulders as he shook her. "Hey! Let her go," Tyler shouted.

The guy ignored him. "You're nothing but a whore." He dropped Candy on her feet in time to slap her again. The blow spun her into a nearby chair. The guy headed toward her.

Tyler got his feet under him in time to grab the guy before he got to her. "Cut it out."

The guy turned. Candy looked more like her mother than her dad, but Tyler had seen that exact expression on her face when she was really pissed off. "You little punk. Fucking my daughter in my own house."

"We were sleeping!" Okay, so he wasn't wearing a shirt, but otherwise both of them were completely dressed. Totally unlike how they were every afternoon between five thirty and six thirty. Good thing her old man never came home then.

"Dad, stop! Nothing happened."

Her father took a step toward her and she cringed on the chair.

"Hey, pick on somebody your own size." Tyler clenched his fists. From the floor, her dad had looked like a giant, but they were about the same height and Tyler had spent the last month hauling wheelbarrows full of cement and bricks around.

"You get out!" Candy's father shouted.

No way. Tyler couldn't leave Candy like this. She looked terrified and it was his fault. Her dad had already slapped her pretty hard. As bad as Tyler's dad was, he'd never taken a real swing at either him, Tiff or Mom. If her dad would hit her hard in front of a witness, what would he do when they were alone? "No."

"Did you just say no to me?" Her father roared.

"Dad, please." Candy stood up. She had a bright red mark on her cheek and a broken blood vessel in her eye was turning it red, too.

"You didn't have to hit her." Tyler's gut clenched. He had said "no" to Candy's dad. This wasn't the way he'd imagined meeting the man.

"I'll discipline my daughter how I see fit."

Tyler glanced at Candy. She was looking at the floor. About two months ago, she'd had a bruise on her shoulder. She said she got it at the store running into a clothing rack. Sometimes she had bruises on her arms, but she said she bumped into things. Why wouldn't he believe that? Brian was the clumsiest person alive. He had bruises all over his arms and legs. Now Tyler had to wonder. They did seem to try not to be in the house together. Had he not been paying attention so much that he hadn't noticed her dad was beating her? Some kind of shitty boyfriend he was. "No, you won't. You can't hit people."

"Tyler, leave it alone. It's okay." Candy's voice shook. She held up her hands and they were shaking, too.

"I'm gonna hit you, you little punk," her father said over her.

Tyler squared his shoulders. "Go ahead. Just don't hit her."

"Tyler," Candy whimpered. She was crying and her right eye was all red now making her look demonic. "Please, just go. I—"

Her father whipped around to glare at her and she flinched, stumbling back into the chair.

"I'm not leaving without her." He licked his teeth. He'd never met Candy's dad before but he'd known dozens of guys just like him. Guys who wouldn't take on somebody who stood up to them, but what if he wasn't one of those guys and didn't back down? Well, working construction did have other benefits. "Candy, come on."

"But—"

He sidled around her dad in the direction of the door and held out his hand to Candy. His car keys and wallet were on the side table so he grabbed them on the way. She climbed over the arm of the chair to stay as far away from her father as she could. Her hand slid into his. She'd made her choice.

"If you leave this house, Candace, don't expect to come back."

Candy looked up at Tyler, tears streaking her face. Then she huddled closer to him.

"You little whore!" her father shouted from the front door as they walked down the driveway. "You really are your mother's child. I have to wonder if you're really mine."

Tyler got her into the car and drove a couple of blocks before he stopped. When he turned to face her, she wrapped herself in his arms as tightly as she could with the steering wheel in the way.

"He was never like that before. I swear he wasn't." She sobbed. "We weren't even doing anything. We were sleeping."

Never? The bruises really seemed suspicious now. She could have said something. "I'll take care of you." What now? She couldn't go home with him and she didn't seem to be up to telling him where any of her friends lived. She couldn't sleep in his car. He needed to get her somewhere safe. Right now, if he knew where Joe lived, he'd take her there. Damn, when the chance finally came to save the day for her, he didn't know how. "We're gonna have to wake up Mr. Dale. He'll know what to do." On the way to Mr. Dale's, Candy was silent. She kept her head on his shoulder as if she couldn't stand to be out of contact with him.

Mr. Dale's house was dark. Tyler had to ring the doorbell four times before the porch light came on and he heard the latch.

"What the hell?" Mr. Dale scowled at them. "Tyler, what happened to Candy?"

"My dad did it." Candy sobbed.

Mr. Dale's eyes hardened. "Come in. Let me get you a cup of coffee."

Once in the house, Tyler held onto Candy until her sobbing subsided again. Mr. Dale brought them cups of coffee and then sat down in the chair rubbing his face. "All right boy, what happened?"

"I took Candy home and she invited me in to watch a movie. We fell asleep, Mr. Dale. I swear."

Mr. Dale glanced at the big blue bowl of condoms he kept on his dining room table then back at Tyler, still shirtless. "How did Candy get hurt?"

"Her dad came home and found us. I swear we were just sleeping."

"So her father hit her?"

"He yanked her off the couch and slapped her really hard and he was shaking her. I tried to make him stop." He clenched his jaw against tears. Boys didn't cry.

Candy pressed her face into his shoulder and he tightened his grip on her. He was never letting her go. "He was never like that before," she mumbled.

"Candy, we're here to help you." Mr. Dale patted her arm. "Tyler, continue."

"He called her a bunch of bad names and hit her again, so I figured we needed to get out of there. I didn't know where else to go."

"Why couldn't you have taken her to your house?"

Tyler shifted in his chair. "You didn't meet my dad at my graduation party."

Mr. Dale nodded. "Enough said. Tyler, you are a good boy and I'm glad you felt you could come to me, but this is a matter for the police."

"No!" Candy jerked away. If Tyler hadn't had such a tight hold on her she'd have fallen out of her chair. "Please, don't arrest my dad. He doesn't mean it."

"They never do. Your father is a dangerous man."

"He's not." She clawed into Tyler's arm. "Please don't let them arrest my dad. I just want to go home."

"I am not taking you back to that lunatic. He hit you and called you a slut. Even my dad never hit me." Just threw stuff.

"I agree with Tyler. Candy, you cannot go back to that environment. You are underage. I should call Child Protective Services."

Candy sobbed again.

"Do you have to Mr. Dale?" Maybe coming here hadn't been such a hot idea. CPS would stick her in foster care who knew where and he'd never see her again. "I have a job. I'll get an apartment. I can take care of her."

"Tyler, you are nineteen years old and she is seventeen. It's too late at night to sort this out. We all need to get some sleep, but I can't have a teenage girl in my house overnight unless I want to be fired from my job and then tarred and feathered in the middle of town." Mr. Dale sighed. He took a drink from his coffee cup and set it aside. "I'll wake up Eleanor Callisto and see if she's got a spare bed."

* * * *

Candy huddled at Mr. Dale's table wearing Tessa's jeans and Connie's T-shirt. Maddy, the Goldman Group's office manager, had accepted her excuse of food poisoning when she'd called off work, but Joe had been on the phone fifteen minutes later wanting to know why, if she had food poisoning, she wasn't at her normal contact number. Then he insisted on coming to rehearsal tonight when she wouldn't tell him where she was.

Last night Mr. Dale had been on the phone with Mrs. Callisto for all of five minutes before he was bundling her into his car. Mrs. Callisto, Jason, and three of Jason's sisters had met them at the door. They'd already made up the bed Jason's oldest sister had left behind when she moved out six months ago. Brian hadn't known about the chaos until Tyler got to work in the morning, but now he was hovering around her like a bodyguard. Tyler stood behind her at the kitchen table holding her hand. She felt like a husk watching Mr. Dale pour coffee for Mrs. Callisto and talk about normal stuff. What the band was doing over the summer. The weather. How her job was. As if there wasn't a crisis holding hands at the table.

Mr. Dale had moved the bowl of condoms off the table since Mrs. Callisto was there. Bear leaned on the kitchen counter flipping a quarter back and forth across his knuckles. Jason stood behind his mother's chair, scowling. Brian leaned against the window running his hands through his hair as if that would help him get a grip on the situation.

When the doorbell rang, Mrs. Callisto jumped. At least they remembered why they were there. Mr. Dale answered the door and Joe's voice rang through the house demanding to know where Candy was. He stormed the room as if he wanted to throw her over his shoulder and carry her away.

"Candy, what happened?" He pulled her out of her chair and inspected her face while glowering at Tyler. "Did he do this to you?"

"No." Candy jerked away from him and retreated to the safety of Tyler.

"Then what happened? Why wouldn't you tell me where you were today? What is going on?"

"Joe, if you'll just sit down." Mr. Dale held out his hands.

"I'm not sitting down until somebody tells me what's going on."

"Her dad beat her up." Jason's jaw flexed.

"Jason, hush," Mrs. Callisto said.

"Well, that explains a few things." Joe sank into a chair. "I didn't think you were that clumsy."

"Clumsy?" Mr. Dale stiffened. "This has happened before?"

"No!" Candy cringed. "Not much."

"Did you know?" Jason shouted at Tyler. "How could you let her stay there when her dad was hurting her?"

"Jason, stop it," his mother snapped. "You're not helping."

"Let's just figure out what to do going forward." Joe pressed his palms on the table. "You're not going back to that house so where are you going to stay?"

"She can stay with me as long as she likes." Mrs. Callisto shook her short, graying hair off her face.

"She's got a year of high school and four years of college ahead of her. Are you prepared for that?" Joe asked.

"I am."

"Are you sure?" Joe's eyes narrowed to diamond points.

"I know this girl better than you do, sir."

Candy admired the way Mrs. Callisto faced down Joe. Not many people would, especially when he went into ferocious mode. Mrs. Callisto should work for him. That way at least one person would be left standing in the conference room when he blew his top.

"Good. Candy, are you all right with that?"

There didn't seem to be any other choice. Dad had said she couldn't go home if she left. She needed her things, though. Clothes. Makeup. Books. Some pictures. "I have to go home and get my stuff."

"No." Joe pulled his credit card out of his wallet and slapped it on the table.

"What's that for?" Candy asked.

"You're not going back to that house. Just buy new stuff."

"I don't want new stuff. I want my stuff." She clutched Tyler's hand, peering up at him.

"Candy, it's not safe for you there." Joe shoved the card closer to her.

"Tyler will go with me."

Joe looked at Tyler and shook his head. "Not good enough."

"Then I'll go too," Brian said. "We'll all go. It'll make quick work."

Joe stared across the table at Jason. "And who's going to keep that one under control?"

"I'll go along to oversee." Mr. Dale turned to look at Joe. "We'll go when we expect Candy's father to be out."

Joe pursed his lips. "That'll have to do. Next issue is emancipation."

"What's that?" Tyler asked.

"I'm not a slave," Candy said at the same time.

Joe leaned across the table, jabbing it with his index finger. "That man has legal rights over you until you turn eighteen, which you won't for almost a year."

"Eleven months."

Tyler squeezed her hand.

"Can we get back to the matter at hand?" Joe asked. "I can call my lawyer right now and have everything drawn up. Get a restraining order thrown on for good measure."

Candy's stomach ground on itself. "My dad isn't a bad guy. He doesn't exactly keep me chained in the basement. Most days I don't even see him. He only loses his temper once in a while and he kinda had a good reason this time. Don't you think?" She looked at Mrs. Callisto. She was a parent. She'd understand what made Dad so mad.

But Mrs. Callisto was already shaking her head. "No, sweetheart. There's no excuse. I haven't raised a hand to my children since they were out of diapers though God knows they've deserved it a time or two." She shot a glare at Jason.

"So it's settled." Joe stood the way he did when he finished a meeting at the office. "I'll call Brad and have him file the emancipation paperwork. Sandy, you and the boys will go with Candy to get her things tomorrow afternoon, after work. Candy will stay with Mrs. Callisto until she's ready to move out on her own."

Mr. Dale gave Tyler a firm look. "Don't get any ideas about the two of you moving in together until she's at least a sophomore in college. You're both too young."

Tyler grumbled. Candy pressed the back of his hand to her lips. He'd suggested three or four times already that they move in together. It wasn't a bad thought if they could afford it, but if Mr. Dale said no, there was no chance.

The doorbell rang again and everybody jumped.

"Who the hell?" Mr. Dale started for the door. Then he stopped. "Marc Wells. Forgot about him in all the excitement."

Mr. Dale let Marc in while everyone crowded into the living room to greet him. Candy hung back. She didn't want to be meeting anyone looking like this. According to Mrs. Callisto, it was going to take a week for the redness to go away in her eye. The bruises on her cheek would take at least as long to disappear. She knew how to cover the bruises on her face with makeup, but the eye? How was she going to go to work like this?

Marc held his guitar case to one side as he looked around the room. He was tall and lean, but a little more broad-shouldered than the other boys. He had presence and knew how to dress himself. "Wow, I didn't realize I was meeting the whole extended family."

"We happened to have something else going on so there's a few extra people here. You don't mind playing for the whole bunch, do you?" Mr. Dale smiled.

"Shit no, I play in front of bigger crowds than this all the time." Marc grinned and started shaking hands. When he got to Joe he stopped. "What a minute. I know you. You're Joe Goldman of the Goldman Group."

"That I am."

"You guys said you had a publicist, but I didn't realize."

"I don't do the heavy lifting. The real work is done by Candy." Joe reached back for her.

Candy cringed. She'd been trying to hide in the background. What was Joe thinking pulling her up front looking like this? Brian turned to her and realization dawned on his face, but he smiled and put his arm over her shoulders to guide her forward. She plastered on a smile for Marc.

He'd been smiling too, but that melted away. "Holy shit, darling. What happened to you?" Candy dropped her gaze to the floor, but Marc caught her chin so he could look at her bruises again. "Are you all right?"

"This is my girlfriend. We're taking care of it." Tyler wrapped his arm around her shoulders pulling her away from Brian.

Marc took a step back. "Yeah, okay. Are we gonna do this thing?"

Tyler let everybody go downstairs ahead of them. "Are you okay?"

Candy shrugged. "I want to go home." Home. Where the hell was home now? Mr. Dale's? Mrs. Callisto's?

He stroked her unbruised cheek with the backs of his fingers. "I can take you anywhere you want."

"Can you take me back to yesterday before all this happened?"

"No because now that I know what was going on I wish you hadn't been there ever. What do you want to do?"

Wanted or needed to do? Running and hiding wasn't an option. "We better go downstairs. They've all seen the damage."

He kissed her before guiding her to the basement. By the time they got there, everybody was in their places. Jason and Brian had glommed onto Marc like worshippers. Mrs. Callisto watched from the couch with a benevolent smile. Joe came over and took her hand.

"Sorry. I somehow forgot you might not want to be shown off tonight."

"It's okay. I have to go in to the office tomorrow. I might as well get used to the attention."

"I was thinking about that. I have some things you can do on the computer. I'm going to have one sent to Mrs. Callisto's so you can work from home for a while."

There was that word again. *Home.*

"We're all in this together, kiddo." Joe hugged her. "You're never gonna be alone."

Candy leaned her head on his chest. Now she knew where home was. Wherever these people were.

* * * *

Mr. Dale was staring at him, ignoring whatever Candy was telling him about the promotions stuff she'd cooked up with Joe. In the two weeks since they'd moved her stuff out of her dad's, her bruises had cleared up, her eye healed and she had returned to the office with Joe where she'd gotten back to work on their marketing campaign.

Jason slapped him on the back of the head hard enough to drive his mouth into the microphone in his hand.

"Asshole," Tyler snapped, wiping his lip. *Blood, fantastic.*

"Language." Mr. Dale raised both eyebrows.

"If you could remember the fucking lyrics." Jason sneered.

"Boys!" Mr. Dale snapped.

"I can remember the lyrics." Tyler slouched. "It's a hard song to sing. Even Joe Elliott says so."

"It's not that hard," Brian said.

"You try it. It's too fu—it's too fast." Tyler rubbed his neck. Two weeks, he'd been sleeping in his car. The day after he'd rescued Candy from her dad, he'd tried to brave his own and gotten threatened with a beer bottle again. Mom said Dad had gotten laid off, and all he did now was sit around the house, drinking. She'd sent Tiff to Gramma Lewis's for the rest of the summer and she was staying at one of her teacher friend's houses. He'd told her he was staying with a friend so she wouldn't worry. "It's a stupid song anyway."

"It's Def Leppard," Jason wailed, as though Tyler had blasphemed.

"So? It sucks."

Jason took a step toward him, but Mr. Dale stood up. "Boys. Tyler, what is the matter? You're off and you've been off for days. Candy is fine so it's not that. What's going on?"

"Nothing I can't handle." His lip throbbed and that wasn't the only body part that was. Two weeks that he hadn't been able to get any time alone with Candy either. They couldn't do anything that couldn't be witnessed by Mr. Dale or Mrs. Callisto. Another week of this and he wasn't going to be able to stand up straight. Either from the car or from the blue balls.

"Obviously it is something you can't handle or you wouldn't be screwing up left, right and center." Marc slid a cigarette out of the pack in his pocket, glanced at Mr. Dale and slid it right back in.

"It's just a dumb song." Tyler scowled at his shoes.

"You loved it when it came out, Tyler. You were the one who wanted to do this song." Candy lifted the mic out of his hand and inspected his lip. Her fingers felt amazing as she brushed the swelling. The mic was off anyway. He was only holding it so he had something to do with his hands.

"You look tired." Candy stroked her fingers across his cheek. "Are you drinking enough water at work?"

"I think he needs some alone time with the little woman." Marc snickered and the others joined him.

Candy blushed and looked at the floor.

"Boys." Mr. Dale sighed. "Okay, band meeting."

The others groaned, but Tyler figured at least it gave him a chance to sit next to Candy while they talked about the marketing and whatever upcoming gigs where confirmed.

When they'd all settled in the living room with glasses of milk and a plate of Fudge Stripe cookies, Mr. Dale asked, "What's going on, Tyler?"

"What? Nothing." This had nothing to do with marketing or gigs.

"Bullshit." Mr. Dale leaned his elbows on his knees. "You haven't been able to sing for a week. You forget the words to everything and you get tongue tied."

"That song is stupid."

"It's not just that one song."

The others all stared at him. Candy leaned her head on his shoulder. He had been having trouble remembering the words and his tongue did seem to be getting in the way a lot. Over the last week, he'd had more accidents on the jobsite than Brian. Some of the guys were threating to wrap him in Tyvek sheeting and stuff him the cement mixer. "My dad got laid off two weeks ago."

"So he's been giving you grief?" Marc asked.

"I haven't given him a chance. I haven't been back to the house."

"For two weeks?" Candy sat up. "Where have you been sleeping?"

"My car."

"Jesus Christ." Mr. Dale jumped out of his chair and started pacing the living room. "You boys will be the death of me. Where is your mother?"

"She's staying with a friend. I told her I was crashing on a friend's couch."

Mr. Dale rubbed his hand through his hair. "And you didn't think to tell us sooner?"

"I was handling it."

"No you weren't." Jason cracked his knuckles.

"Will you stop doing that?" Marc winced, glaring at Jason. "It's not a problem. You can surf my couch until something changes. Problem solved. Let's just break for the night. You need to get your head in the game for the show tomorrow." He stood up and stretched.

Candy took Tyler's arm and held him back as the others went downstairs to collect their things. "Why didn't you tell me?"

"I got you kicked out of your house the same night. Taking care of you was more important." He swallowed. The same night even. Wasn't she a lucky girl to have him? She'd be better off with Brian.

"You didn't get me kicked out. I had to get out of there one way or another. Dad was escalating."

"You should have told me he was hurting you."

"I didn't think it was a problem."

"I didn't think not being able to go home was a problem for me."

She frowned and nodded. "Mr. Dale still isn't going to let us move in together."

"No." *God, living with her would be heaven.* Even in a crummy little apartment, as long as they were together. Fall asleep with her every night and wake up with her every morning. Then he could be her hero. He swept a lock of hair off her cheek. "I miss you."

"I miss you, too. There's got to be someplace we can go. There's that no tell motel on Hawkins." Her eyes were warm and hopeful. How he missed that.

"I don't want to get you shot." He kissed her forehead. It made his swollen lip flare, but the rest of him felt pretty good about the move.

The thunder of the rest of the band coming up the stairs forced them apart.

Mr. Dale draped his arm over Tyler's shoulders. "Don't keep these things to yourself in the future. No matter what the problem is, we can solve it together. We're a family." He dropped his other arm over Candy's shoulders. "Right?"

Yeah. Family. And because they were family, Candy was starting to feel more like his sister than his girlfriend.

* * * *

Candy had her books and notes spread out on the conference room table. Spring finals were next week, she was ending her first year of college, and Touchstone had half a dozen important gigs coming up. She hadn't been able to go to rehearsals for the last two weeks because she'd been too busy. Tyler had come by the office bearing dinner every night, but that was the only time she'd gotten to see him. Now that he was living with his mom and sister in an apartment across town, it was the only time they could be together at all.

Joe leaned in the door. "You okay?"

"I'm fine."

"Yeah, you look like you're about to implode." He strolled in and turned one of her textbooks over. "Econ. My favorite." He flipped the book back over like seeing the cover gave him nightmares. "In two weeks I have to go to LA again for some meetings. You in?"

"LA? You want to take me to LA?"

"Time to really get your feet wet, kid."

Candy frowned. "But I can't. I have finals."

"This is after finals, dingbat."

Her frown deepened as she tried to grasp the concept of "after finals." Last summer after graduation, she'd had a two-week break before she started summer classes. One actual year in college and she almost had enough credits to be a junior, but it meant she hadn't stopped working.

"Hey, you in there?" Joe knocked on her forehead.

Candy blinked. "What do you need me to do in LA?"

"Follow me around. Take notes. Look pretty." Joe shrugged. "Nothing you don't do naturally."

"Okay, why are you taking *me*?"

Joe sat down in the chair next to her. Finally. The truth. "I'm trying to woo a big client. A music management company. They're looking to add a publicity team to their menu of services and they need to know we know what we're talking about. I don't, but you do."

"I know how to publicize one local band."

"You have the basics. Plus, you look pretty."

"I'm arm candy?"

"Sort of, but not really. I want this client. You are uniquely experienced in what they are looking for. This is not charity, darlin'."

"And how many people in the office are going to hate me for getting this perk?"

Joe leaned back in his chair. "In this business, if people don't hate you, you're doing it wrong. Besides," he raised his voice so it would carry into the hall. "A few people around here need to get off their asses and get some real clients. Local hair salons and dental offices do not cover the lighting bill."

"Somebody's in a mood today," Candy muttered.

"Hey, when it's your office, you can run it any way you like. I prefer to use fear and intimidation. You in for LA or not?"

"I'm in."

"You're in for what?" Tyler asked. By the look on his face, he'd been standing at the door for more than just the last line. He had a bag from the deli around the corner in one hand and two Cokes in the other. His hair was still wet from the shower.

"I'm outta here." Joe walked out.

"Joe's taking me on a business trip." Candy wrapped her arms around him.

"To Los Angeles." Tyler's voice was flat and hard.

"Isn't it exciting?"

Tyler licked his teeth. "I can't stop you."

"Come on. You should be happy for me. He wants me to do this because of all the work I've done for you and the band."

"I'm thrilled." He pulled away from her and set the bag on the table.

"Tyler."

"Why should I be happy? I've hardly been able to see you for most of the last year and the first chance you get you're going away with Joe." He folded his arms.

"Like we're going to have any time together anyway. You have three hours a day between the time you get off work and the time you go to rehearsal."

"And you scheduled classes for most of that time all year long."

"It was one class and it was the only time it was offered. I can't take the classes when they're not offered and I needed that class to get my fall classes."

"Jason sees more of you than I do."

"You say that like it's a treat for me." Candy put her fists on her hips.

"We haven't been able to have sex for weeks."

Candy glanced at the door. Tyler didn't have to pitch his voice to carry into the hall. He did it automatically. "Tyler, please, let's not fight about this now." She put her hands on his chest.

Tyler lifted her fingers to his lips and closed his eyes. "I miss you. I want to be with you all the time and I never get to see you."

"I think about you all the time, too." She shivered. His lips were so warm and soft on her fingers. The last time they'd had any time alone was over spring break. On the last day, they'd gotten a hotel room. That was seven weeks ago.

Tyler pressed his lips to her palm. "Every night when I go to bed I think about being wrapped around you. I'm going to get an apartment. I want us to live together."

Live together? Now? Was he nuts? "Tyler, we can't. We promised Mr. Dale."

"We promised Sandy we'd wait until you were at least a sophomore. You had enough credits to be a sophomore at the end of fall term." Tyler stroked her cheek. "Candy, I want to be with you all the time. I want to marry you."

Marry? He was nuts. "But how would we live? Neither of us makes enough money, especially not with my tuition. We've got to think about this, Tyler."

"But you'll think about it?"

Candy swallowed. "I'll think about it."

"That's all I ask. I can make you happy, Candy. I know I can."

* * * *

Tyler watched the shifting panorama of girls backstage. He'd seen Candy off on her big trip the day before yesterday. Mr. Dale had abruptly decided to visit some friends for the weekend right after Candy's finals ended so they had his house to themselves. That helped burn off some of Tyler's horniness, but not all of it. Surrounded by hot chicks, and he couldn't have any of them.

Brian dropped onto the couch next to him.

"What's wrong with you?" Tyler asked.

"Fuck off." Brian drained the beer bottle in his hand and dropped it on the floor.

Tyler followed Brian's gaze. Jason's sister Tessa was making out with Marc across the room. That explained it.

"Women suck," Brian snarled.

"I wouldn't mind having one sucking on me right now."

Brian laughed.

Tyler scanned the room. Jason had a girl with him. Bear had two. There were mobs of girls hanging around. Girls with boyfriends. Girls with girlfriends. Girls who would cheerfully go either way, all the way, and every which way. And he had a girlfriend in Los Angeles who would *think* about marrying him. "I asked Candy to marry me before she left."

"What'd she say?" Brian asked. Then he flinched. "Yeah, dumb question. Sorry."

"Me too. I've been dating her for two years. More than two years. You wouldn't think she'd have to think about anything. By now it should be automatic."

"I know. It's like I said. Women suck."

"Is there another beer over there?"

Brian passed him a bottle. It was warm and nasty but better than nothing. They only had about ten minutes before they went out for the last set anyway. Once that was over, they'd tear down, head home, get a couple hours sleep and start all over again tomorrow at Rockin' On the River. An endless grind. Candy was right. He worked all day the entire week and had three hours between work and rehearsal if they didn't have a weeknight gig. Then all weekend, the band gigged. The only full days off he'd had since he joined the band had been the day his parents' divorce came through and the three days he'd had the flu last fall. But that didn't really count because he didn't remember a lot of it. Candy worked part time at Joe's office and took a full load of classes. Sandy had been knocking on doors to get the band a recording contract, but so far, nothing, even with the radio play Candy got them.

"Do you think it's worth it?" Tyler asked.

"What?"

Tyler gestured at the room. Graffiti covered walls, sagging, stained couches, Tessa making out with Marc, crowds of people who were their so-called friends, crap beer, and legal and illegal smoke. No free time, no privacy.

"Hell, yeah." Brian pursed his lips. "I think so."

"You think so what?" Bethany draped herself on the back of the couch around Brian. Tyler bit back a smile at what Candy would say about how Bethany was dressed. Electric green skirt slit up to her hip. Sheer black blouse. Black lace bra. A section of chain held closed with handcuffs as a belt. He didn't even need to check to see if she was wearing fishnet stockings and high heels because she always wore fishnets and high heels. Claimed it was her trademark. He'd have to tell Candy about it when she called tomorrow.

"Just wondering if it's worth it."

"I can make it worth it for you." She flicked open the buttons of Brian's shirt and started drawing designs on his chest with her fingernails, painted to match her skirt.

Tyler stared at her long green nails scraping across Brian's skin. That would feel so good. Everybody said she was amazing in bed and everybody knew from firsthand experience. Brian leaned his head on her belly, smiling blissfully.

"Maybe you should come to my place for an after party." Bethany slithered into Brian's lap and started on his neck.

Fuck. Candy was thousands of miles away. Tyler shifted because watching was becoming painful. Why wouldn't Candy move in with him? He was gonna marry her. Then he'd be able to wake up next to her every day and this shit wouldn't bother him. Tyler stood up and walked out of the room. The bar was loud, dim and smoky. As much cigarette smoke as he ended up sucking down in bars, he ought to start a pack-a-day habit. The DJ was playing Sarah McLaughlin's "I Will Remember You." Was the whole fucking universe trying to rub his nose in the fact that his life sucked?

All he wanted was Candy. Full time. But she was out in fucking California with her boss who'd been making her dreams come true since he met her and could treat her like a princess. They'd flown business class and had dinner at some fancy restaurant. They were staying at Joe's California place because he had enough money to have more than one house. Woo-hoo.

A girl leaned in to shout in his hear. "Hey, what are you doing over here by yourself?"

Tyler checked out the owner of the voice. Cute. Not dressed like a whore. Long straight hair. About the same size and shape as Candy. If he closed his eyes… "Just taking a breather before the last set."

"You guys are really good. I've been to every one of your shows and I've been calling the radio station and requesting your song like every hour."

"Thanks. We need about two thousand more like you."

She laughed with a high-pitched nervous ring. "So listen, I don't usually do stuff like this."

"Talk to people?"

"No." She giggled again and swatted his arm. "I just really think you're hot."

And I have a girlfriend. He knew he should say it out loud, but his mouth wasn't cooperating.

"I kinda wondered if you were busy after the show tonight." She slid half a step closer.

I have a girlfriend in California. "No, just going home to get ready for tomorrow."

She slid the other half step so her body brushed lightly against his. "I could help you get ready."

A girlfriend in California who, when I asked her to marry me, said she had to think about it. "Maybe you could."

* * * *

Seconds after he climaxed and rolled off her, the weight of making a terrible mistake crushed him into her mattress. "I gotta go." He lunged off the bed, grabbing his jeans off the floor. Candy was going to kill him.

"Okay," Jennifer rolled over. "You were awesome."

"Uh, thanks. You too." He yanked his jeans up, his underwear balled inside the left leg. What the fuck was he supposed to tell Candy? He shoved his jeans down to get his underwear and realized he was still wearing the fucking condom, too. He pulled it off and looked around for a trash can.

"Just drop it on the floor." Jennifer stretched on the bed, arching. "I wish you didn't have to go so soon."

"I gotta get home." He zipped his fly and grabbed his shirt.

"See you at the show tonight."

Oh, crap. Tyler ran down the stairs of her apartment to his car. Who had seen him leave the bar? Nobody. After the encore, he'd changed into street clothes and ditched his stage gear with Connie, who was filling in for Candy while she was away.

If Candy had been where she was supposed to be, none of this would have happened. He'd have been standing in front of her in his underwear and there would have been no chance for him to walk out the front door with some chick he'd just met who looked just like her.

Dammit, dammit. Tyler started his car and drove home. Mom and Tiff were asleep. He crashed on the couch without unfolding it. His mother commented on that in the morning, but not on the fact that he was wearing his jeans while his underwear was on the floor with his shirt. He bailed without eating breakfast and drove out to an area of the park nobody went to where he cranked Live's *Secret Samadhi* album. Jason and Marc had students all day. Bear worked in his dad's garage on Saturdays. Brian or Sandy might be home.

Who was he kidding? If any of them found out, they would kill him. Sandy liked to talk about how they were family and they'd deal with things together, but even family had limits. Candy was the greatest and he'd just cheated on her. And Brian? Candy would leave him for Brian. The two of them were tight. Brian would never screw up like this. Brian really could be her hero.

She could never find out. Nobody saw him leave with Jennifer. It never happened. Done deal.

But that night at the gig, she was there. Tyler stopped singing the second he saw her, but they were in the middle of a last choral section and he'd recovered by the time he had to deliver the closing line. Naturally, they would be closing the encore with Def Leppard's new hit "Promises." The lights went down giving him a precious couple of seconds to get his shit together before they came back up for the final bows. The audience screamed. Jason moved into position next to him. Marc on the other side. Lights up. Final bow.

She was still there. Standing at the edge of the crowd smiling like the crowd was screaming for her.

"What the fuck happened to you?" Marc snarled as they walked off stage.

"I forgot the lyrics." He needed to get to Jennifer and tell her to disappear.

"What part of 'I won't make promises I can't keep' and 'ahhhh ahhhh ahhhh' did you forget?" Jason asked.

Tyler veered away from them toward the audience.

"Where are you going?" Connie shouted. "You need to change."

Tyler kept going until all their voices were lost in the song the DJ had put on when the show ended. Jennifer was still standing on the edge of the lighted dance floor. She didn't look anything like Candy. What had he been thinking? She wore a short black skirt and a blue top with black nylons and black shoes. The whole outfit was uninspired. Candy always dressed so much more…finished. "Hey. What are you doing here?"

She stroked his sweaty shirt. "I told you, I've seen every one of your shows. You were great." She bit her lip. "So, what are you doing now?"

"I'm busy. I gotta get changed and stuff."

"You gonna be able to come by my place again after? I had a great time last night." She slipped her fingers under his shirt, stroking his skin.

It felt good, but she still wasn't Candy. "Listen, I have a girlfriend."

She blinked. "You what?"

"I have a girlfriend. Last night was kind of a mistake for me. I'm sorry." He put his hand on her shoulder. "I really need you to be cool with this."

Her jaw flexed and her chest started heaving. "You're an asshole, you know that?" She spun on her heels and stomped away.

Dammit. He didn't need her telling him he was an asshole. He already knew. Tyler turned back toward the dressing room.

Tessa stood five feet away. If anything, she looked angrier than Jennifer. She couldn't have heard over the music, but she looked as if she understood. She shook her head and walked away.

Candy would be home in three days. Somehow, in the next three days he needed to find a way to make this right. because there was no way Tess wouldn't tell Candy the second she saw her.

Chapter 5

Candy wandered through the offices, looking at the pictures on the walls. Tyler would go nuts. Anybody who was anybody had either been here or wanted to be. She wasn't sure who Joe had an appointment with, but he didn't need her for it and this was her reward for landing the management company contract. Now she was really going to be able to figure out how to promote Touchstone. When they did get a recording contract, she'd be ready.

She started reading her way down the gold records lining one hallway. Would it be tacky to take a picture of herself standing under them? She peered up and down the hall. Nobody around. If she worked fast— She got out her camera and tried to line up a shot.

"You'll never get it that way."

Candy jumped, fumbled the camera, and dropped it.

"Here, I'll get it." Before she could stop him the tall, lean boy had snatched up her camera. He had a shaggy but expertly cut mop of light brown hair and round blue eyes. "Shift over a bit. A bit more. There. Say seventh heaven."

"Seventh heaven." Candy laughed in spite of herself.

"One more for luck." He clicked the shutter again and handed the camera back.

"I didn't think there was anyone here."

He shrugged. "I blend into the background pretty good. What are you doing here?"

"Waiting for my boss to get out of a meeting."

"Ah, I'm waitin' for the old man to get out of one. How much trouble do you want to get into?"

"None." Who was this guy and why was he lurking around a record company? He looked vaguely familiar, but she couldn't place the face.

He laughed. "Come on. Have a little adventure. Did you know there's an old recording studio in the sub-subbasement of this building?"

"There is?" He had a weird accent too. It sounded as if he couldn't decide whether he was American or English, which was either really pretentious or really cool. He seemed more cool than pretentious.

"Yeah. Hopelessly outdated so they never use it anymore, but you expect Frank Sinatra to walk in any second."

"That sounds cool."

"You wanna see it?"

"I don't know. Is it okay to go down there?"

"Nobody's going to stop us." He held out his hand.

Candy bit her lip. He was way cute and carried himself with utter confidence, but Tyler... "I have a boyfriend."

He shrugged. "I have a girlfriend. I just want to show you the sites. Nothing like seeing it new again through someone else's eyes. I'm Ricky by the way." He held out his hand.

"Candy." She shook his hand.

"So we going to look at this deserted and possibly haunted studio or what?"

Ricky had more charm than ten men should legally be allowed to have. He took her down in the elevator to the basement and then down two flights of stairs. Two guards saw them, but he just waved and told them where they were going. The guards waved back making her wonder if maybe he was the son of the owner or something.

"Wow, it does feel like Frank Sinatra is going to walk in any minute." Candy ran her hand over the soundproofing on the walls. Against one wall was a standup bass with an ugly crack in the neck and a couple of ancient looking mic stands.

"All the old boards are still in here. I think it would be cool if somebody brought some new equipment down here to do some recording. A guy who used to work down here as an engineer told me sometimes you can hear the fault grinding in playback."

Candy pulled her hand away from the wall. "Is it safe?"

"As safe as anywhere. Give me your camera, I'll take some pictures."

She handed him the camera and posed under his direction. Occasionally, he'd arrange her, but his touch was very businesslike.

"You are a great model. Working with you is like working with my sister. You ever do any modeling work?"

"No." Either his sister was a model or he was that attracted to her. *Whatever*.

"How long are you going to be in town? I'd love to get some shots of you with my camera."

"I don't know." Candy glanced around the room. Way down in the sub-subbasement, nobody knowing where she was. This might not have been the brightest idea. "My boss is probably looking for me."

"I'm not talking about now. I mean tomorrow or something, if you're not busy." His eyes lit up. "You could come out to the house."

"I really should get back." Candy started backing toward the door. He still had her camera, but that would be a small loss.

"Ah, and she freaks out right on cue." Ricky shifted his weight to one leg and tossed his head. "There's about thirty people in this building who will swear I'm not a serial killer or a rapist."

Candy stopped. She shouldn't take his word on it, but for some reason she did. "Well, I'd have to talk to my boss. I'm really out here on a business trip."

"Business trip? Are you older than you look or are you some kind of prodigy?"

Candy shrugged. "I don't know."

"Let's go find him."

"I don't want to interrupt if he's in a meeting."

"Trust me, that won't be a problem." Ricky ushered her back upstairs.

Joe was standing in the atrium, scowling until he noticed them getting out of the elevator.

"Hello, Joe. Meeting over?"

"Yeah. You found a friend."

"Joe, this is Ricky. Ricky, this is my boss, Joe Goldman."

Ricky held out his hand and Joe shook it as if they were equals. "I was hoping I could borrow your assistant for a little while."

"Borrow her?" Joe's eyebrows shot up.

"I'm into photography and the camera loves her. I'd love to get some shots."

"Sure, you want to take her now?"

Candy tensed. Joe was going to let this strange boy just take her away. What was wrong with him? Didn't he even want to know who Ricky was? A last name maybe? Mr. Dale would never do this. "Joe!"

"Trust me, you'll be fine." Joe patted her shoulder. "We don't have anything planned tonight, but we have another meeting tomorrow morning at ten that might take all day and we fly out the day after. Tonight is your only chance."

Tonight? She wasn't ready for tonight. Did Joe honestly think she was going to run off with this person she'd just met? Not that she didn't trust him, but this wasn't rational. Like making over a random boy who walked into her section at the store wasn't rational.

"Dad's going to be busy for a while yet. I can get us a ride home and bring you back to wherever you're staying by seven. I'll even spring for dinner, no strings. Deal?"

Candy glanced at the clock over the reception desk. Two thirty. Four and a half hours with this total stranger? But her gut told her it was the right thing to do. This boy had the run of a major recording company. He, or his dad, might be in the position to help Tyler. She checked Joe's expression. He had that predatory gleam in his eye he only got when he was about to make a major deal. "You sure it's okay?" she asked him.

"Kid, you are exactly where you're supposed to be." Whatever that meant.

Ricky asked the receptionist to get him a car and tell his dad he'd gone back home. They were in the backseat of a chauffeured car heading, literally, for the hills in half an hour. He asked a lot of questions about Tyler and Touchstone and when she played the demo for him, he said it was good, but raw. They needed, he claimed, a good producer and named a few names Candy recognized from major hit albums.

His dad's house was mammoth. She'd been impressed by Joe's condo, but this place had gates and a gatehouse from which a good-looking Hispanic man waved.

"Jorge, our caretaker," Ricky explained. Then he pointed out Luis, the gardener, who apparently lived in a different building at the back of the property. With his family.

Who was this guy? And who the hell was his dad?

"Come on in. I'll grab my camera. The light is amazing at this time of day. Hello Sharon. Sharon, this is Candy. I met her down at the offices. Candy, this is Sharon, she's our cook. Is it going to be a problem to have one more for dinner?"

"You little pest." Sharon smiled. "Of course not. Nice to meet you. I was planning pork chops and applesauce. Is that all right with you?"

Candy nodded.

"Great. Let me go get my camera." Ricky ran up a set of stairs at the side of the kitchen leaving Candy to look around.

The huge kitchen had stainless steel everything and a stove the size of a compact car. The counter tops were golden marble and the rustic table could have seated ten. Callisto's apartment, where she lived with five other people, would have almost fit inside it. Sharon had turned back to the counter where she was peeling apples. People made applesauce fresh?

Ricky rushed out with his camera. "Come on. I don't want to miss the light."

"Ricky, you watch out for critters!" Sharon shouted after them.

"What critters?"

"I don't know. Sharon has been warning me about critters since I was a little kid. I used to think they were monsters. Let's start over here."

She followed him to one corner of the garden. Maybe his dad did own the record company. "This must have been a great place to grow up."

"Well, yeah, when we were here. We live in London part of the year and here and sometimes we go to our place in Greece. And Dad has an apartment in New York."

"I would love to go to London. Or New York." Or anywhere. "This is the first time I've even been out of Indiana."

"Lean on this tree." He positioned her, critically adjusting the angle of her head. "You should go. It's pretty fabulous. Everybody should see Abbey Road Studios once. It's an amazing space and it's right in the middle of a neighborhood where you wouldn't expect. Leighton's house is right around the corner too. Don't move."

Candy had gotten used to the "don't move" line. He alternated between that and "try not to look like you hate me so much." He shifted her from one tree to another and then to a granite elephant statue he said came from India and then to the edge of a reflecting pond. And into the pond. Luis came to watch and shook his head as she kicked off her shoes at the edge of the water and waded around the lily pots at Ricky's direction.

The light was disappearing behind the mountains when Ricky decided they needed to go all the way to the back of the property where there was some scrub. He settled her under a spindly bush, gave the standard lines and backed up to take his shots.

"Your boyfriend's band is pretty good." He snapped a couple of pictures. "I'll see if I can get Dad to listen to them."

"Thanks." Whoever his dad was, that had to be a good thing. Ricky had been very careful to not make any promises beyond dinner and driving her back to Joe's condo when they were done. Tonight when she called Tyler she'd have something to tell him that wasn't going to annoy him.

"Dammit, the light's all gone." Ricky looked up at the sky. "Hey, maybe I could take some pictures of your boyfriend's band. The picture you've got is okay, but it looks like it was done by a portrait photog. Move back a little."

Candy slid further back under the bush. The band picture looked as if a portrait photographer did it because a portrait photographer shot it. Part of a deal she'd worked with Joe's blessing. Something pinched her. She twisted around to see if the bush was attacking her and felt another pinch on her leg. "Ow!"

"Quit moving around."

Candy jerked as burning poke stabbed her right at the line of her bra. "Ow. Something's biting me."

Three more stings erupted under her shirt. Candy jumped up and yanked her shirt over her head. "There's something in my clothes." Another sting at the top of her thigh.

"What is it?"

"I don't know," Candy wailed.

Ricky grabbed her arm and pulled her away from the bush. "Red ants. We don't have red ants in the yard."

"Make them stop!" Candy got her jeans open and tried to kick them off without taking off her shoes. Ricky attempted to catch her before she fell over, but she landed hard on her hip.

"Okay, calm down. Calm down." He skimmed his hands over her skin, flicking off the tiny red ants.

"I can't calm down. It hurts."

"Don't scratch it."

Shivers took over her body. She hugged herself. The bites were starting to itch as well as burn.

"What's going on?" Luis crunched through the bushes. "Ricky, what have you done?"

"I didn't do anything. Fire ants attacked her."

"Well, they live out here, Ricky. You know that."

"But they don't come in the yard."

"Of course they do. Did you think they obeyed the property line?" Luis put his arm around Candy's shoulders and she sobbed. "Come on, we'll take you back to the house."

Her jeans were twisted around her ankles and wrapped around her shoes. Luis picked her up and carried her. Candy buried her face in his shoulder, the humiliation burning as bad as the bites. Another couple of seconds and she'd have had her bra off, too.

When Luis carried her through the door, Sharon said, "Holy crow, what happened?"

"Fire ants. Many bites."

"Ricky! I told you to watch for critters. Take this and go fill the guest room tub with warm water. Put in three cups."

Candy didn't see what Sharon handed him because Luis was settling her in a chair at the table. Sharon started untangling her shoes from her jeans. Luis left so at least she didn't have to be half naked in front of him anymore.

"You poor dear. You are breathing all right. How are you feeling? Do you feel sick or dizzy?"

Candy shook her head. "No, but these really hurt."

"I know they do. You must have ten. We'll get you into a Borax bath and that'll draw the venom out."

"I can't believe I stripped off my clothes."

"Trust me, it's the best thing you can do. Those little suckers crawl in until they can't go any further and then they sink their nasty little mandibles into you. Just don't scratch them because that makes it worse." Sharon helped her to her feet. "I'll run your clothes through the washer to get rid of any ants that might still be in them. The bathroom is right down the hall there and down the stairs. Check the bites while you wash up and make sure there aren't any little ant pieces left in them. There's some Benadryl in the cabinet. Go ahead and take some, it'll help with the swelling. Ricky! You get out of the way!" she shouted down the hall.

Candy found the bathroom and stripped off the rest of her clothes. There were no more ants in them she could see, but there was a large welt forming on top of her right breast and another under it, one more on her stomach, four in a row right at the top of her left thigh and two on her back. She swallowed the Benadryl dry before sinking into the warm bath. Immediately, she felt better. The burning and itchiness died away. She lay in the water trying to figure out how she was going to salvage this situation.

Whoever Ricky's father was, she needed the connection for Tyler. After this, Ricky was either going to want to distance himself from her or he was going to feel bad and try to make it up to her. The latter would be perfect, but chances were good he'd want to forget he ever knew her. So when she got out of the tub, she was going to have to play it cool. Like getting mauled by vicious ants because he didn't pay attention to what was in his own fucking backyard didn't bother her. The things she did for Tyler.

When the bathwater cooled to uncomfortable, Candy climbed out and wrapped herself in the white silk bathrobe on the back of the door.

Stepping into the hall, she heard voices from the kitchen. As she got closer she heard a voice like honey saying, "Ricky, you should have been paying attention. You know there's fire ants out there. What would you have done if she'd been allergic?"

"Come on, Dad. I didn't think there were any in the garden. Luis said he got rid of them."

"They're insects. They creep back in."

Maybe if she rescued Ricky from his dad, he'd be grateful and help her out. All she had to do was say she should have been paying attention, too. Easy peasy. Candy stepped into the kitchen and her mouth dropped open. All thoughts of playing it cool and rescuing Ricky from his tyrant father vanished.

Ronnie Bauer. Ricky's father was Ronnie Bauer. Why hadn't somebody warned her? Christ, she was standing in Ronnie Bauer's kitchen wearing a borrowed bathrobe. "Um, um."

Ronnie turned and it was as if the sun was coming out from behind the clouds. He had a lot of impact on TV and records, but in real life, it was like being run over by a semi full of raw charm. "Hello, Candy, how are you doing?" He reached for her hand and when she didn't extend it, he leaned down to take it. "Fire ants are a bitch, but Sharon knows what to do. She said you had ten stings."

"I—I." Candy glared at Ricky. "You jackass. Why didn't you tell me your father was Ronnie Bauer?"

Ricky shrugged. "I thought everybody knew who Dad was."

"Everybody does, but that doesn't mean everybody knows you're his son."

Ronnie laughed. "I think she's recovered. You ready for dinner? Your clothes are still in the wash, but Tanya has some things around you can borrow. You look about her size. She won't mind."

Tanya? Tanya Bauer? The model Tanya Bauer who was also Ronnie Bauer's child?

"Ricky, show her where your sister's room is so she can get dressed and we can have dinner. I'm starved."

* * * *

"Why didn't you tell me that was Ronnie Bauer's son?" Candy wailed when she walked through the front door of Joe's condo.

"Because I knew you'd freak out and not be able to do your job," Joe wailed right back before setting aside his drink. "How did it go?"

"Fabulous." Candy settled on the footstool in front of him. "Ronnie said he's been talking to the record company about starting up his own boutique label using their distribution and he likes Touchstone. He called Jerry Eland who's going to listen to the demo and decide if he wants to produce them."

"That's great. Who's Jerry Eland?"

"I have no idea, but Ricky was very excited about it."

"What happened to your clothes, because that's not what you were wearing this afternoon."

"I got attacked by fire ants and Sharon washed them. These are Tanya's."

"Tanya Bauer?"

"Yes."

"Mercy." Joe picked up his drink. "Before you give them back I want to rub my face on them."

Candy stood up. "You are a dirty old man. How bad do you need me tomorrow?"

"Why?"

"Ricky wanted to know if I could hang out and I thought it might be a good way to cement the relationship."

"You really are a quick study." Joe grinned. "I love it. Go ahead. Maybe you can get him to kiss your stings and make them all better."

"I don't think so. I love Tyler. I'm not going to cheat on him."

"No matter how rich and famous the next contestant is?"

Candy folded her arms causing a couple of her ant bites to flare up, but she didn't want to show weakness in front of Joe. "Exactly."

* * * *

Tyler went straight from the job site to Candy's office. They'd gotten in from LA this morning and she'd said they were going to the office after dropping off their stuff. Jason had started doing a Snoopy dance as soon as Sandy got off the phone with Jerry Eland last night. Tyler still couldn't believe Candy had stumbled into Ronnie Bauer's son while hanging out at a record company. Maybe she'd fucked him. Then Tyler wouldn't have to feel so guilty about Jennifer.

Except he doubted it. Candy would never cheat. No matter what.

There was a parking spot right in front of the building so he took it and waited. Everybody in the band knew. Tessa had been flapping her big mouth before he even got to the dressing room Saturday night. Jason told him he was an asshole. Bear told him if he couldn't keep it in his pants he shouldn't have a girlfriend. Brian had wanted to know how he could possibly cheat on such a great girl as Candy. Marc just smoked a cigarette, staring and not saying a word. Tessa had yelled at him the entire time he was changing while Connie muttered behind her. Thank God, the usual gang of hangers on had been shut out because they all knew and liked Candy, too. The next morning Sandy had left a message with Tyler's mom that he was disappointed, which his mother agreed with. Awesome having your mother know you cheated on your girlfriend with some random bar girl too. But if he could get to Candy first, he could confess and make it right before anyone else poisoned her against him.

Candy shuffled out of the building and headed straight to the car. She slumped into the passenger seat without kissing him. "I am so tired. We got on the plane at seven California time, which is like four regular time and flew for five hours. We landed here at nine local time, dropped off our stuff and came straight to the office for an eleven o'clock meeting. And then, I had to start on all the stuff that didn't get done all this last week because Joe and I were gone because apparently Joe and I are the only ones who actually do any work around here." Closing her eyes, she lolled her head against the back of the seat.

Good news, she hadn't heard about his mistake yet.

Bad news, this wasn't the time to tell her.

She opened her eyes. "Jerry Eland called Mr. Dale. What happened?"

Jerry. She was already using the guy's first name. He was probably some super hunky, filthy rich beach bum who would sweep her off her feet. And after what Tyler had done, she'd be happy to go. If he were a good guy, he'd be happy to see her go, but obviously, he wasn't or he wouldn't be in this mess. "Yeah, he called last night. Somebody's sending contracts to us."

"That's fantastic! Ronnie said he sounded really excited about working with you. He's got some plans already for things he wants to fix about you."

"Fix?" Jesus, she was calling Ronnie Bauer by his first name too. Another guy who could sweep her away. He could never measure up to these guys in the hero department. All he had was his youth, enthusiasm, and loyalty. *Oh, wait.* Tyler's stomach churned. "What do you mean fix?"

"To make you a little more commercially appealing." She patted his arm.

"I thought we sounded fine."

"You do, but we listened to the demo yesterday and Ronnie was pointing out some things like—I don't know. I could hear it when he said it, but I can't explain it. Just be professional and take the criticism. Jerry wants to make the best possible album and so does Ronnie. He might even drop into the studio to help. Touchstone is going to be the first jewel in his record label crown."

Fantastic. Now he not only had to hear about how wonderful Joe was, but he got to hear about how wonderful Ronnie Bauer was. And Ronnie Bauer really did walk on water.

"I've got a surprise for you." He squeezed her hand.

"Oh honey, I don't know if I'm up for a surprise tonight. I'm so tired."

"This won't take long." If she was that tired, she wouldn't come to rehearsal. She might go home to bed before Tessa could get to her. Then he wouldn't have to tell her about Jennifer until tomorrow. Unless Tessa got her in the morning before she left for class. He'd better work it in before either rehearsal or she ditched rehearsal. Maybe over dinner. "I want to show you something before we go get dinner."

"All right." She closed her eyes. "Let me know when we get there."

It wasn't far, but she fell asleep before he stopped in front of the big white house with black trim on a quiet street off the main road ten blocks from her office and fourteen blocks from campus. The bus stop was right around the corner making it easy for her to get where she needed to go until they could afford to get her a car. "Hey Candy? Wake up."

"What? What is it?" She looked at him and then at the house. "What about it?"

"That's my apartment."

"Your apartment?" She scratched her head. "What do you mean?"

"I rented the attic of that house. I'm going to live there. It's got a little kitchen and a private bathroom. I move in next week."

She stared at the house, frowning and blinking. "Why are you moving out of your mother's?"

"Because it's impossible for us to be alone together."

"But you're going to be going away soon to record."

"I know, but that could be months from now."

She sighed. "Did you sign a lease yet?"

"Yeah. I thought you'd be happy." He reached for her hand. "We don't have anywhere we can be alone. Now we can come back to my place. It could even be our place. You could move in with me." She didn't want to marry him, but that didn't mean she wouldn't want to live with him.

"You know, I'm too tired to make sense of this. Can we talk about it tomorrow?"

Tyler dropped the car into gear. "I thought you'd be happy."

"I'm tired," Candy snapped. "I've been up since very early this morning and worked all day. And I worked all week."

"I'm sure it's backbreaking following Joe around. I worked all week too and I have to get up early every day." Tyler jerked the steering wheel, turning the car around.

Candy opened her mouth and then shut it and turned to stare out the side window.

Probably a bad time to hit her with any news. He should have taken her to eat and then home and showed her the apartment tomorrow when she was rested. But then when would he have gotten his confession in? This argument sounded a lot like the ones his parents had had. His divorced parents. He reached for her hand. "Candy, I'm sorry. I missed you a lot and I've been missing you a lot even though you're right here."

"Yeah, it shows." Candy sniffled.

"I did and I'm an asshole. I know you work hard. You did what nobody else has been able to do. You got us a recording contract. And we're going to be going away to record and then we're going to have to tour for something like forever and I'm going to miss you. I'm just edgy, Candy."

She turned, pulling his arm around her shoulders so she could lean on him and sob. "I don't want to fight with you. I love you."

"You're tired and it's been really stressful. It's okay now." He stopped at the intersection and kissed the top of her head. "Everything is going to be okay now. Let's get a pizza and head to your place." Nobody should be home now. Jason had lessons until right before rehearsal and Tessa had work most nights and studied at the library all the others.

Except when they arrived at Callistos' with pizza, Jason met them at the apartment door and Tessa was sitting at the table, studying. She jumped up before he'd gotten all the way inside.

"Did he tell you?" Tessa demanded.

"He told me. Where's my suitcase?" Candy asked.

"I took it to your room for you." Jason walked out of the hall. "Good trip? You are awesome."

She smiled. "Thank you."

Jason picked her up and swung her around. "Do you realize the only more powerful person you could have found us was Paul McCartney? I can't believe you bumped into his son roaming the halls of the record company. You are amazing."

Tyler ground his teeth. He should have asked Jason what to do. So far he'd handled the whole welcome home thing a thousand times better and they'd just walked in. Lucky for Tyler, she was much more likely to leave him for Brian.

"Yeah. I tried to get him, but he didn't happen to be roaming around the offices when I was."

"Next time, try harder." He set her down and gave her a smacky kiss on the cheek.

"I can't believe you're not more upset about this." Tessa put her fists on her hips, her scowl deepening.

"I'm not happy about it, but what can I do now?" Candy sat down on the couch.

Tyler broke in before Tessa could say anything more. "I got enough for everybody." He slid the pizza box on the table.

"Oh cool, double meat." Jason dropped down beside the coffee table.

"How can you be so calm about this," Tessa shouted.

"Tessa, drop it," Jason said. "Candy's not upset."

"I'd be upset if my boyfriend was fucking another woman."

Candy had been lifting a piece of pizza to her lips. She had been perfectly calm. He had been about to get away with keeping it from her for another day.

Until Tessa opened her big fucking mouth.

"Jesus, Tessa, will you shut up!" Jason shouted.

Tessa screamed something back at him, but their fight reduced to feedback for Tyler. He was watching Candy.

Candy sat frozen for a long time. Then she very slowly put down her pizza, keeping her eyes on the table. She licked her lips. It seemed to be about a week before she spoke and then she was so quiet he couldn't hear her over Jason and Tessa. Then she turned her gaze to him. "Well?"

"Well what, baby?" His head was empty. No good reasons, bad excuses, or pathetic pleas for forgiveness. Nothing at all for the woman who loved him so much she was making his dream career come true.

"Did you…do what she said?" Candy's eyes were huge, begging him to say it wasn't true.

Tyler opened his mouth to deny it, but nothing came out. Jennifer had been pretty and there, and he'd been lonely and stupid. She'd understand it was a mistake. He'd never do it again. He didn't want anyone else. He'd…slipped.

"Oh my God!" Candy jumped up and ran for her room.

Tyler chased her and pounded on the door. "Candy, let me explain. Come on, baby. Open the door."

Nothing.

"Candy, come on. I screwed up. I'm sorry. It only happened once." He pressed his forehead on the door. "I missed you so much when you were gone and I was so lonely."

The door whipped open so fast he nearly stumbled into the room. "Are you saying it's my fault?"

"No."

"You said you missed me and that's why you did it." Her eyes were red and her face was streaked with tears, but she looked so calm.

"It's—well—what I meant was you weren't here and she looked just like you and I wanted her to be you."

"But she wasn't me and you did it anyway."

"You were out there having sex with Ricky Bauer."

"I was not." She folded her arms.

She wouldn't. Never in a million years. He needed another tack. "Candy, I'm sorry. I was lonely and I screwed up and I will never do it again."

"I don't understand how you could do it the first time." Candy blinked and tears slid down her cheeks. "I thought you loved me."

"I do."

"But if you love me how could you *make love* to another woman?" She brushed her face like the tears embarrassed her. "I could have. I thought about it. Ricky is really cute. Even before I knew who he was, I thought he was cute and I wanted to, but I told him about you."

Tyler hung his head. "I'm an asshole. I wish I had a decent excuse, but I don't. I wanted you and I couldn't have you so I settled for the next best thing. It was a mistake. A terrible, horrible mistake. You have to give me another chance." He got down on his knees. Now he knew how that skeleton in Mrs. Creedy's bio lab felt with the wind blowing through his ribs. "Candy, please. I'm begging you."

"Tyler."

"I just want to be with you." He'd have been better off if he'd been Mrs. Creedy's skeleton. Every bit of him burned as if it had been soaked in gasoline and lit by a stray match. "Please, Candy."

"Tyler, stand up."

"Not until you forgive me and let me have another chance."

"Tyler."

"I can't live without you."

"You seem to be very capable of finding replacements." She shut the door in his face.

Chapter 6

Candy stood in front of the desk facing the boys lounging on the two hotel room beds. She ran her finger down the list of appearances and interviews she'd arranged for them over the next few weeks. Sandy sat at the desk beside her with a copy of the list he'd been making notes on as she spoke. Brian and Jason had blown a condom up like a balloon and were batting it back and forth between the beds. Marc was examining his fingernails. Bear had a muscle car magazine open in his lap.

Tyler looked fine. Well rested. Healthy. Not in the least unhappy or still missing her two years later, he was playing solitaire on the table by the window. Why didn't he feel hollow inside? How come he didn't lie awake nights trying to figure out how to go back?

"Looks great, Candy. You're a marvel." Sandy stood up and kissed her cheek. "Thanks for coming out here."

"I had to take care of some business at the LA office for Joe so it's not out of my way." Candy closed her notepad. "I'll look at the itinerary for the last month of the tour and see what I can do about getting you some local interviews."

Sandy drew a breath and the boys stopped what they were doing to stare at him. "I'm not sure we're going to be off the road when we planned."

"What?" Jason shouted. "Sandy, you promised. We've been on the road for eight months and before that we were in the studio for six."

"I did no such thing. I promised you and your parents that we'd get through this tour in one piece. Ronnie feels with the album breaking the way it is, we need to press our advantage and headline."

"Headline." Marc sat up. "We're going to headline?"

"Yes. You'll have a one-month break at the end of March to rehearse a longer set and then we're on the road headlining." Sandy beamed at them.

The boys jumped up high fiving one another. Tyler grabbed her and swung her around. Then he set her down and turned away as if she didn't matter to him. Brian started singing "Back In the USSR," so Jason grabbed a guitar and played the song. Before long, they were singing in a drunken, off-key caterwaul their fans would have never recognized.

Candy swayed before Sandy put his arm over her shoulders. He gave her a tight smile as if he understood that she felt like a snow globe. Guiding her out of the room, he yelled over his shoulder, "Get out of the minibar. You have sound check in half an hour and you don't need to be drunk for it." Outside, he turned her toward him. "How's Joe doing?"

All the hollowness she'd felt before filled abruptly with greasy oatmeal. Her head pounded. Had the nurse remembered to fill his hot water bottle? She forgot last time and he caught a chill he couldn't shake for hours. "He's fighting."

"It's that bad."

It wasn't a question, but Candy nodded anyway. She hadn't known Sandy when his wife, Ellen, was losing her fight with cancer.

"I'm so sorry. Chemo is the worst part. Once this is over, you'll really be able to see how he is." Sandy hugged her. "You're a good girl, Candy. Are you going to be free for dinner with me before we leave town?"

He'd talk about the boys, about Tyler, which would kill her slowly. "No, I have to have dinner with Joe's office manager tonight so I can give her a thorough reporting."

"I know this isn't how most college kids are spending their last few days before graduation."

Candy shrugged. "I had all the hours the end of last semester, but I forgot to file the paperwork to graduate. I'm really already done. Joe just wants to see me walk the plank."

"I'm proud of you." Something crashed inside the room. "I better get back in there. You take care of yourself."

"I always do."

"No, you don't." He patted her shoulder and swiped open the door. "What was that noise? Brian, get off the table." The door closed behind him, cutting off his words, but not the rumble of his voice.

Candy rode down to the lobby. Dozens of girls loitered, trying to get up to the floor the band was on and one very irritated security guard held them off at the elevator bank. A couple of them accosted her wanting to know who she'd done. She fended them off until she could get to her car,

Joe's car, and leave. They wouldn't believe it anyway. And since the story about dinner with the office manager had been a lie, she had no plans for the evening.

She should have said she'd have dinner with Sandy, horrible dinner conversation topic or not. Anything was better than being this alone.

What she shouldn't have done was break up with Tyler. Cheating or not cheating, anything was better than being this alone.

* * * *

Tyler hung back as Sandy pushed everyone out of his room.

Sandy scowled. "What do you want?"

"You were talking to Candy. How is she?" Tyler could feel the tension wrapping around his vocal cords. It started the second Sandy said she was coming last week. He'd gotten to touch her for two seconds. He should have gone in for a kiss. Too late for that now, but he could live on the sensation of having her in his arms again for weeks.

"As good as can be expected trying to take care of Joe by herself."

"And how's Joe?" He regretted every single time he'd cursed the other man. They'd be nowhere without Joe and nobody deserved what he was going though.

"Dying, but they're doing everything they can for him." Sandy folded his arms. "Why don't you talk to the girl?"

"I tried. I got down on my knees and begged and she shut the door in my face."

"That was almost two years ago. Things have changed."

Tyler clenched his teeth. Girls were everywhere out here. As many as he wanted. As many as he could handle.

None of them were Candy.

* * * *

The phone didn't wake her. She was used to getting up at six at home which was three California time so she'd been staring at the ceiling for a while. But the panic didn't know what time it was. She snatched the phone off the cradle whispering, "Please, not Joe, please not Joe."

"Hello?"

"Hi, baby. I miss you." Tyler's drunken slur didn't soothe her fear. It just replaced it with something else. Something needier.

"Tyler, how did you get this number?"

"Baby, you would be amazed at what I can get." His self-satisfied tone disappeared when he spoke again. "I miss you."

"Tyler, you've been on the road for eight months. You miss everything."

"No, I miss you more than anything. I missed you before I left."

"You're drunk and you woke me up." Candy sat up in bed.

"That was the only way I could talk to you."

He had to be drunk to talk to her. "By getting drunk and calling me in the middle of the night?" Candy rubbed the sheet between her fingers. Joe only had eight hundred thread count sheets. They made butter feel rough, but they were so cold.

"I couldn't talk to you today. I wanted to. I wanted to tell you how sorry I was about Joe. I wanted to tell you I was sorry. I am. I'm still sorry."

"Tyler."

"I really mean it. Really, really. I miss you and I love you. I can get anything I want and all I want is you."

Candy closed her eyes, energy draining out of her. Wasn't this what she'd been waiting for? "I miss you, too."

"Really?" There was a pause. "Come to the hotel. Tonight."

"It's four in the morning." Candy swung her legs over the side of the bed. This was stupid. Insane. She needed to stay away from Tyler as much as possible to protect her own sanity.

"We roll at ten. This is the only chance we're going to have to talk face to face. Please." His voice dropped to a soft, irresistible growl. "I need to touch you."

"Tyler."

"Please."

Candy chewed the inside of her cheek. "I'll be there in an hour. Tell the desk so the guard will let me upstairs."

"Thank you, Candy."

He said the same thing when he opened the door of his room a little under an hour later right before he buried his hands in her hair and kissed her. There was no sign of drunkenness in his touch, just a desperation that she wanted to believe was for her.

He picked her up and carried her to the bed. His arms were so strong. Within them she was safe from everything. When he slipped his hand under her shirt, cupping her breast, she moaned his name. Since they broke up, she'd been dreaming about this moment, stretching underneath him again, and the reality was so much better. He stripped her naked, tasting her body before driving into her. Distantly, she heard the headboard of the bed rapping on the wall, but the rest of her senses were tangled up in him. Strong, safe, and loyal. He'd always been there and he'd always be there.

Afterward, she curled her head on his chest.

"All I ever wanted to do was get back together with you," he murmured. "I missed you every second."

"I missed you, too." She kissed his bare skin. In all the months since they'd broken up, no other man had attracted her attention. They'd tried. Lots of them. Guys in her classes. Guys at the office. Clients. She'd signed men to the agency because they hoped to stay on her radar long enough to catch her personal interest.

They'd never have succeeded. Her attention was always fixed right here. But what about his?

"Have there been other women?"

"Other women? Sure. Lots. None of them meant anything to me though."

Lots. She hadn't been able to bear the thought of another man touching her and he'd been drowning his sorrow in groupies. "How many?"

"Aw Candy, do we have to talk about this now?"

Candy sat up. She knew that tone. Postponing the inevitable. The mobs of women downstairs. At least a dozen had been lurking around the lobby when she'd gone through. "How many?"

"A lot. I don't know. I wasn't keeping a scorecard." He reached for her shoulder. "Come on, baby. None of that matters now. Not if I have you back."

"But what if you get bored or lonely? How can I ever trust you?"

He shrugged. "I don't know. It's not like I really care about any of them anyway and they know it."

Candy pulled away from him. "What?"

"Don't do this, Candy. Not now."

"No, I want to know what you meant." She did and she didn't. Her gut felt like a Molotov cocktail.

"Jesus." He climbed off the bed. "Candy, on the road, screwing a groupie isn't about love, it's about entertainment."

Candy wrapped her arms over her breasts. She had asked. She could have kept her mouth shut. "Am I entertainment?"

"No, don't be stupid." He knelt on the foot of the bed. "I love you."

"But if you love me, how can you be with other women?"

"Because I spend twenty-two and a half hours a day waiting to sing. I get thirty minutes for sound check and sixty on stage and God help us if we go a second over because the guys in Ground Force have started being the biggest assholes on the planet since the audience started leaving after we go off stage. Like it's our fault they're a bunch of has-beens. They're getting a bigger slice of ticket revenue anyway."

Candy pursed her lips. "But you'll stop with other women if you're with me."

"Sure, if you were on the road with us. Come tour."

"I can't. Joe's sick and I have to run the company for him so he can focus on getting better."

"So we have sex with whoever we want when we're apart. As long as it's not somebody you like, I don't care. Sex and love are different. I love you. Sex is just scratching an itch."

That sounded a lot like something Bear would say. She could hear them now. A bunch of immature boys justifying their bad behavior to one another on tour buses and airplanes. "Why can't you sleep alone when I can't be with you?"

"Don't ask me to do that. It's the only fun I get to have. Sandy gets totally irate about drugs and he controls the amount of liquor we can get. We got the promoter to bring us some more about a month ago and he threatened to quit. He's convinced we're all gonna end up dead in a pool of our own puke."

"Maybe that's what I should do."

Tyler frowned. "What? Become an alcoholic?"

"Quit."

"What are you talking about?"

Candy crawled off the bed and grabbed her jeans.

"Candy, what are you doing?"

"Quitting."

He snatched her shirt off the floor before she could get to it. "What are you talking about?"

"Give that to me." Candy pulled the shirt, but he wouldn't let go. "Let go."

"I will not. What do you mean, quit?"

"Find yourself another publicist. Find yourself another girl to fuck. I'll send one up." What had she been thinking coming here? He had grown up all the sudden? He could magically be faithful? He'd changed?

"Will you stop being nuts?"

"I'm not being nuts. Now give me my goddamn shirt!" Candy shrieked.

"Hey." Someone banged at the door. "What's all the racket?"

Brian, world's biggest doormat.

Candy let go of the shirt and ran for the door naked from the waist up.

"Don't!" Tyler ran after her, but she got to the door first and yanked it open.

"What the—holy shit." Brian stumbled back. "Sorry. Didn't mean to interrupt."

"Brian, I need a shirt."

Brian reached to pull off the one he was wearing before he realized he wasn't. "I can—um—in my room." He pointed to the open door beside Tyler's. One more wide-eyed look and he dove through it. Candy grabbed her purse from the dresser.

"You are not going anywhere until I talk to you." Tyler tried to block the door.

Candy dodged around him. The door across the hall opened.

"What the fuck is going on?" Jason demanded. "Candy, why are you half-naked?"

"Because I'm quitting."

By the time Candy got to Brian's room the rest of the band, a half-dozen girls, and Sandy had spilled into the hall. There were two more in Brian's room.

"You guys gotta go," Brian told them.

The girls shrugged, grabbed their stuff and left, still dressing as they did. Jason crowded in with Sandy behind him. In the hall she could hear Tyler arguing with Bear and Marc.

"What is this shit about you quitting?" Jason demanded.

Brian handed her a shirt, which she pulled over her head, and over her purse requiring her to pull her arm out of one of the sleeves to disentangle herself.

"Candy, calm down before you do something rash." Sandy held up his hands.

"I already did something rash." Candy tossed her purse on the bed where it landed on the corner and spilled all over the floor. "Fuck."

"Slow down." Brian gathered her stuff off the floor and put it back in her purse. "You're getting all wound up."

"I have every right to be wound up," Candy screamed.

"So do we," Jason shouted back. "You can't quit on us in the middle of the night."

"Jason, will you shut up?" Sandy snapped. "This is not the time or the place. Now what happened?"

Candy covered her face with her hands. Her head pounded louder now and her chest felt like the bass drum in the middle of Bear's solo. Tyler was still shouting in the hall with Bear and Marc. It sounded as if Marc was inventing new curse words for exactly how stupid he thought Tyler was. Bear might have been too, but his voice was much lower so only the essence of his fury reached her. Brian said something to Sandy. Then the sound was cut off by the closing door.

Brian put his arm around her shoulders. "Come sit down. You want a cup of coffee? They always leave some packets of instant in the rooms." He guided her to a seat on the end of the bed before moving away. She heard him in the bathroom running water. Every sound had the acute ring of physical touch. The running water. The clap of the top of the kettle. The rumble of voices in the hall.

"So I guess you're still in love with him," Brian said.

Sobs broke from her chest.

"Oh come on, don't cry. Jeez, I'm sorry." Brian wrapped his arms around her shoulders. "Look, Tyler's a jerk. We're all jerks. But I know he still likes you."

"Obviously not as much as I love him. I wouldn't need another man."

"Yeah." Brian stroked her hair. "I'm sorry, Candy."

"You understand, don't you? You understand that I need to get away from him. I can't see him. I want him so much and I want him to love me and he doesn't."

"He does. It's just, there's all these girls and there's not much else to do."

"It's not fair."

The kettle clicked off.

"I know. None of it's fair. You want that coffee?"

"No, I'm so tired."

"Why don't you sleep here tonight?"

"I'm not having sex with you, Brian."

"I know you're not. We've done the brother speech already. You're tired. Things have been rough with Joe and your school and stuff. I know you want to throw Tyler under a bus right now, but if you do that, you do it to all of us. We're your friends, too. Let's sleep on it and in the morning we'll get some room service and talk it over when you can think. I won't be able to contribute much though. You were always the smart one."

Candy leaned on him. All of them helped her move out of her dad's house and surrounded her those first fragile weeks after. She had been living with the Callistos until Joe's chemo forced her to move in with him. When Joe was diagnosed with cancer, they'd all called every day for the first few weeks trying to find out what was going on. Bear and his brother found her a car and Tony was still maintaining it for cost. Marc had been following along her classes, helping her study. Within a week after they met her, they'd trusted her to pick out their stage clothes, cut their hair and arrange all their advertising. They were the only family she'd ever really had. "I'm really tired, Brian."

"I know, Candy. We'll get some sleep and figure it out in the morning. I promise."

* * * *

"What did she say?" Jason demanded as Brian climbed onto the bus. He looked like shit, but no worse than Tyler felt. All night after they'd let him go back to his room, he'd listened at the wall with a glass trying to hear anything.

"She isn't quitting, but she won't be meeting us in person anymore. Not all of us." Brian slouched into the couch. "She'll send us what we need to know."

"And how's she doing?" Bear asked. Their driver climbed on and started the engine.

"She's tired and depressed and confused." Brian shrugged. "The usual cocktail."

"You are such a dick, Tyler." Marc shook his head.

Tyler pulled his knees up to his chest and wrapped his arms around them. They were just girls. *Why couldn't she understand?* It wasn't like he loved them or they loved him.

"She said Joe isn't responding to the chemo the way the docs hoped. It's pretty bad. He's only working on like half a lung or something now and she said the docs are afraid it's spread to his liver. She hasn't told him because she wants to keep his spirits up."

"Shit. He was fine when we started this tour." Bear shook his head.

"That's the way it happens." Sandy sat down as the bus started moving.

Tyler peered at all of them over his knees. When she said she'd come to the hotel, he'd thought he had it made. Now he was a huge moron. A huge, lonely moron.

As miles ground away under the wheels, the others drifted off to other things leaving Brian open.

Tyler settled on the couch beside him. "Hey." *What happened last night in your room? Did she cry? Did she talk all night? Will she ever give me another chance? I need to know everything.*

"Hey." Brian kept staring out the window.

"So—"

"Look, I know what you're going to ask."

Did you have sex with her? Tell me she didn't have revenge sex with you. If it was anybody else I wouldn't care, but you. She likes you. It would mean something if it was you.

"And I don't think you're an asshole." Brian rubbed his face. "Candy's being totally unreasonable. She can't expect you to be totally faithful like that. It's not fair. But she's my friend too and her feelings are really hurt. She hardly stopped crying all night. I didn't get any sleep."

She wouldn't. Not with Brian. Not with anybody. She was too loyal.

"The whole situation sucks." Brian heaved a heavy sigh. "Really sucks. But nobody thinks you're an asshole. I'm gonna go take a nap." Brian shuffled back to the bedroom.

None of the other guys were looking at him, let alone glaring at him like he was the world's biggest jerk. Maybe Brian was right. In a couple of years maybe Candy would listen to reason.

* * * *

Candy leaned across Helen Wheals' desk to look at the list of travel immunizations the older woman had gotten from the public health office. "Are you sure you don't mind doing this?" Candy asked. "It's not really your job description."

Helen kept her eyes focused on her list. "I'm happy to do it and the new computers are already doing a lot of the billing and invoicing I used to do for Joe. I have to do something to justify my pay. How's he doing?"

Candy smiled. "He's doing really well. This California sun is good for him. You should give him a call."

"I will." Helen rattled the paper in her hands. "I think we should talk to the boys' mothers and get their childhood shot records."

"Why?"

Helen looked up. "Some of those things you were immunized against when you were babies are still running rampant in other countries. We don't want the tour to be derailed because they come down with measles. It's a system we should have in place if we run tours for any other bands."

"All right. I'll get in touch with their mothers about the shot records. Thanks tons for getting this together for me." Candy stood up.

"No problem. I sent the band's account records to Sandy three days ago, but I haven't heard back from him."

"He's pretty tired. I believe he landed about midnight. The boys have a one-week break between shows. Bear's brother picked him up at the airport."

"All right, I won't panic yet." Helen held out the list.

Candy stood. "Thanks again." She took the list and walked out of Helen's office. On the way down the hall, she was stopped three times by the three teams competing for the Crest account. Everybody told her she was crazy to tie up half the agency's resources chasing one client, but this was a big client and Joe was backing her. Once she arrived in Joe's old office, she closed the door and stood staring at his desk. It was glass and chrome and she hated it. His desk in the office back home was oak. She much preferred it, but the sun here was good for Joe. She slid into his black leather chair that still felt too big and surveyed the list. They boys were not going to be happy about all the shots. The tattered phone book she'd been carrying since high school had settled to the bottom of her purse, but it was current.

Connie found Jason's shot records while they were on the phone. Mrs. Callisto was very organized. She promised to drop off a copy at the local office of the Goldman Group.

Marc's mother sounded hammered but swore she remembered him getting all his shots before he started school. She promised to look for the records. Candy made a note to call back tomorrow. Maybe if she tried earlier in the day Marc's mother wouldn't be at the bottom of a bottle.

Mrs. D'Amato kept Candy on the phone while she rooted through the attic for Bear's baby book. She wanted to know everything that was going on, but she was as impressed with mentions in the local paper as with heavy rotation on MTV. She meant well and she found Bear's shot records in Tony's baby book.

Brian's father promised to leave a note for his mother. Candy didn't doubt that Brian had had all his shots or that his mother would deliver copies to the local office.

Leaving Mrs. Franklin. Candy lifted the phone from its cradle and dialed without looking at the number. They hadn't spoken since she and Tyler broke up three years ago.

"Hello?" The voice on the phone was too young and too bored to be Tyler's mother.

"Hi Tiff, it's Candy Perry."

"What do you want?"

"Is your mother home?"

A heavy sigh and the phone clanked on the other end. Candy knew Tiff had started college the previous fall. Tyler was paying for it just like Jason was paying Tessa's law school tuition. Those bills were among Helen's many duties.

"Candy! Hello. It's so good to hear from you." Mrs. Franklin sounded breathless. "How is everything?"

"Hi, Mrs. Franklin."

"I thought I told you to call me Angela."

"Yeah, that was a while ago. I guess I forgot." The first time she met Tyler's mother had been at his high school graduation. Tyler had been wearing jeans and a dress shirt that Candy had picked out for him. Candy had been wearing a pale blue sundress and white sandals. His mother had walked over to her, smiled and hugged her telling her what a great influence she had been on Tyler while Tyler blushed and rolled his eyes. Then she'd told Candy to call her Angela and that she hoped to see a lot more of her. Five years later and this was probably not what Angela Franklin had meant. "I was calling about Tyler's immunization records."

"What for?"

"The boys are going to Japan and Korea on tour and we need to make sure they stay healthy. There are immunizations they're going to need to go overseas, but we wanted to make sure they'd had all the standard childhood shots while we're at it."

"Oh, dear."

Candy leaned into the phone as if hearing better would throw some meaning on what Angela had said. "I'm sorry?"

Angela sighed. "Tyler has never liked getting shots."

"Does that mean he didn't get his mumps and measles vaccinations?"

"No. He got them, but I don't know where the records are. It was traumatic for everyone." Heavy sigh. "He doesn't like shots. Or hospitals. Or doctors much."

Candy scratched her neck. In the past five years the band had had a number of medical brushes. The time Brian fell off the stage. That other time Brian fell off the stage. When Jason slipped on the edge of a hotel swimming pool and hit his head going down. Marc had had bronchitis at least three times and several sinus infections. Bear fell off his drum riser in the middle of a show. He also fell off the top of the tour bus once and no one had determined what he was doing up there in the first place. Dozens of slips, sniffles and drunken accidents that had landed four of the five members of the band under the care of a physician. Never Tyler. "Is this a phobia?"

"He hasn't been diagnosed."

Of course he hadn't. He didn't like doctors. Great. "Well, thanks for the warning. If you can find a vaccination record for him, we'd like to have it on file."

"Not a problem. It's been so lovely to hear from you. I hope you're doing well."

"Yeah." Candy turned the chair to the window so she wouldn't be facing the door. The view out the window was of another office building. "I'm fine. And you? Tiffany doing well in school?"

"Tiffany? She's fine. It's been an adjustment."

Candy nodded. "Well, it was good talking to you, but I have work to do."

"Feel free to call anytime."

"Certainly, Angela. Goodbye." Candy hung up. Tyler's mother had to be blowing the whole thing out of proportion. Brian was super clumsy, Bear drank too much, and Marc smoked. It put them at greater risk to hurt themselves. Tyler happened to be the most graceful one in the group. That's what kept him healthy. Not some imagined fear of needles.

* * * *

Tyler watched Candy and Sandy talking as if he was watching a ping-pong match. He hadn't taken in anything they'd said for the last ten minutes because he stopped processing when Sandy mentioned immunizations.

"We can go to our family doctor, right?" Brian asked. "At home?"

Candy looked at the paper in her hand as if she hadn't heard. She'd meet with the band now, but she was doing her best to pretend they weren't there. It had taken a year to get her inside the same room with him and it wasn't enough.

"I can get someone to come in and do it. I think if you guys are going to tour outside the US, you're going to need immunizations." Sandy frowned. "I don't like this hepatitis one. It's going to take some time and we're running on a short schedule."

"They only need the first two injections before exposure." Candy glanced up from her notes. "They can do the other one any time within six months after the first two."

Tyler wiped sweat off his forehead. *Three shots over six months?*

"Japanese encephalitis?" Sandy asked.

"Helen talked to a doctor about that and he said unless the guys were going to be out in the country, they won't need it. They won't be going out of Tokyo or Seoul."

"Good, that will eliminate one."

Tyler glanced at the other guys. Bear was poring over a car magazine. Marc, chewing on his pen, had a newspaper open to the crossword. Jason was twiddling a pick between his fingers. Only Brian looked at all concerned with the conversation, and he wasn't interested in stopping it.

"Typhoid fever? In this day and age?" Sandy asked.

"It was on the list, but the doctor Helen talked to said it was unlikely and we could skip that one. I did talk to the guys' moms and they dug up their shot records from when they were babies to make sure they'd had all the vaccinations. Helen thought we better check."

"Clever woman that Helen. One of these days I'm going to hire her away from you," Sandy muttered. "If we ever get to have an office to put a business manager in."

"Tyler?" Candy said.

Tyler swallowed hard trying to work out the knot in his throat.

Candy stared at him. "Are you okay?"

The fact that she'd acknowledged him should have been exciting, but he couldn't remember why. They were going to make him go to a hospital. Germs. Needles. People died in hospitals. "Fine," he whispered.

"Your mom said she knew you'd had your MMR when you were a kid, but she can't find the records. I think we should have a blood test to make sure. We'd rather you didn't pick up the measles on tour."

"No." Tyler clenched his fists.

Sandy looked up from his paper. "No what?"

"I don't want to go."

"To the doctor or to Japan?" Sandy frowned.

"Japan. I don't want to go. Cancel the tour."

"Cancel the tour?" Marc threw down the crossword puzzle he'd been working. "Have you lost your fucking mind?"

"No, I think it's a waste of time." Tyler jumped out of his chair.

"Wow, Japan is a waste of time? What have you been smoking?" Jason muttered.

"Tyler! Have you been smoking? You know it'll damage your vocal cords. And whatever it is better be perfectly legal." Sandy glared at Marc.

"What? I swear my cigarettes are just cigarettes and I'm trying to quit." Marc threw the newspaper on the floor and stormed out of the room.

"You have all been in little rooms together too long." Candy set aside her pencil. "Tyler, why don't you want to go to Japan all the sudden? You were all for it six months ago when we discussed it."

"Well, I've changed my mind." Tyler headed for the door. Marc had the right idea. Too many small rooms for too many months. They were suffocating him.

"You can't do that," Jason shouted after him.

Tyler paced down the hall to the ice machine. The first tour had been incredible. Too damn long, but incredible. Except for the breaking up with Candy. Then they were six months in the studio working on the second album, which was slaughtering all the sales figures from the first one.

"Hey man, what's up?" Brian, the last person he wanted to talk to, asked.

"I don't see why we have to tour all the time." Smoking seemed to calm Marc down. Maybe he should give it a try. The Beatles smoked. Weed was good, too. Sandy hated anything and everything that smacked of drugs, but how bad could weed be? Damn, most nights he walked off stage with an excellent contact high.

"Because that's how we make our money and keep our fans happy. Besides, you love performing." Brian grabbed his arm. "Can you slow down? If I wanted a workout, I'd go to the gym."

"Then go. I'm not stopping you."

"Tyler?" Candy caught him as he passed the door of the room they'd been meeting in. Great, now he had Brian and Candy out here. "Tyler, what is the matter?"

He swept past her. There was a cigarette machine in the lobby. He could call down and have somebody bring a pack up for him. On his next circuit, Candy had stepped into the middle of the hall with her arms folded. When he tried to dodge around her, she stepped in front of him again. The next attempt was just as successful. "Will you let me past?"

"No. Not until you tell me what's wrong."

She was so beautiful. Way back when he met her, she'd been hot, but time gave her something else. Something way beyond the expertly tailored gray suit whose jacket she'd left in the room or the expensive haircut. Would she listen to reason now? Could he make her understand that he really loved her and none of the other girls meant anything?

"Tyler?"

"Come on, man. Tell us what's wrong," Brian asked.

"Just fucking go away!" Tyler shouted at Brian.

Brian flinched. "Dick." Then he stomped into his own room. Before the door slammed, Tyler could hear Brian's current steady groupie, Bonnie, asking what was going on.

"Tyler," Candy said softly. "He's trying to help."

Was that what he was doing when he took you to his room before I could talk to you last year? Helping? With friends like that who needs enemies? I could have straightened it all out if they'd just given me the time.

"Why don't you want to go to Asia? When we started talking about it before the tour started you were all excited to play the Budokan like the Beatles and now all the sudden you don't want to go."

"Maybe we've been working too damn much, huh? Shit, we've either been on the road or in the studio for three years now and we've got a couple of months left in this leg before we go to Europe. I don't even have a home anymore. I live out of suitcases."

"It's the nature of the beast. You knew that when you signed on. Besides, I know you. The only time you're really alive is when you're onstage."

Because when he was onstage, somebody loved him. When he was offstage, nobody did. "I miss you, Candy."

Candy took a step backward. "Let's stick to the topic."

"Why can't this be the topic?"

"Because you're tired and upset about something and you're not making rational decisions."

"Damn." Tyler leaned on the wall.

Candy stepped forward again and put her hand on his arm. "Tyler, why don't you want to go to Asia?"

"Why don't you want to talk?"

"Because you're using it as an excuse to not talk about why you don't want to go to Asia. We are not having a relationship discussion because the relationship is over. We are having a business discussion because we are still in business together and Sandy is tired of dealing with you guys."

"How's Joe doing?"

"Remission and you're off topic again. We were talking about the tour. It is going to tack another three weeks on to your travel time, but in the greater scheme of things, that's not so long and you stand to gain a lot. Not to mention what you stand to lose by backing out of the contracts." She chewed her lips. "We were talking about the vaccinations for the trip. Is that what's bothering you?"

"Why do we need them? Can't we just go?"

"It is the vaccinations." Candy leaned on the far wall and started laughing.

"What is so fucking funny?"

"I've just spent months holding Joe's hands through hundreds of needles in two rounds of chemo and you're afraid of a couple of immunizations."

"I'm not afraid."

She stared at him.

"I don't like needles."

"I see that. What can we do to make it easier?"

"Drug me?"

"I think that might mess up the vaccinations, but we can ask."

Talk to me? Tell me you love me? "Will you hold my hand?"

"Hold your hand?"

For the sensation of her fingers around his again he could face any monster. "Like you did for Joe. I know it's not the same, but it would make me feel better." *Especially if you said you loved me. If you'd give me another chance.*

She sighed. "The things I do for you boys. All right. I'll hold your hand if you'll promise to go to Asia. Let me go tell Sandy so we can schedule it."

Tyler watched her walk back into the room. At least she wasn't pissed at him anymore. She'd somehow shut down the part of her that loved him. If he asked nice, maybe she'd tell him how she did it, because the part of him that loved her was still a gaping wound no needles were ever going to get closed.

* * * *

"What did he say?" Jason asked.

Candy surveyed the hotel room. Three years later and another hotel room. This time all the boys were paying attention. Probably because Sandy wasn't there to pay attention for them. They'd been upgraded in that time, too. Now, instead of two double beds, they rated a suite. Sandy really shouldn't be touring with the band anymore. Now that they had an office in L.A. he could hire a tour manager and hand off some of the responsibility. Then again, if the boys were going to be this irresponsible, they might solve that issue themselves. "He said he wasn't going to bury anyone else and he wasn't going to be responsible if you guys were going to get yourselves killed."

"We're not going to get ourselves killed." Bear sulked. "We were having some fun. We never get to have fun anymore."

Candy leaned on the desk. "God, Tessa is right. This is like dealing with a bunch of kids."

"We're not kids. We're all legal age." Bear started rolling a Coke can between his fingers making the aluminum crackle.

"Which is why you called me in a panic three days ago because Sandy quit and walked out on you. And, may I remind you that there is no legal age for heroin? That's illegal for everybody."

"It was a party. The guys in SendDown were having a party." Bear crumpled the can in his hand and started pressing it flat with his fingers. He had a wall of pop cans on the bus.

"The guys in SendDown are always having a party. Their drummer hasn't been sober in six months."

"Can't you talk Sandy into coming back? We can't trust anybody else." Marc pulled a cigarette out of the pack in the nightstand and broke it.

"Okay, let's get this straight. Sandy started being your manager because he was your high school business math teacher and he knew you were going to get screwed over and screwed up. He promised all your parents except Marc's that he'd keep an eye on you and make sure you were safe."

"He's not our teacher anymore."

"He's still your designated responsible adult. None of you seem to be ready to take up the job." Candy snuck a glance at Tyler, but he was picking threads out of the comforter and hadn't had a word to say yet. "Plus, the last time we saw each other was over an open grave."

"Joe died of cancer," Brian pointed out.

"The last time before that was over an open grave, too."

"My mother drank for years. Cirrhosis and emphysema were neck and neck." Marc rubbed the back of his neck.

"That doesn't change the fact that Sandy has had to bury four people in the last eight years starting with his wife. He's not going to bury anybody else if he can say anything about it."

They all had their mouths open to protest, but she held up a hand to stop them.

"Tessa ran the death rates for various narcotics and for musicians. Old age isn't the top cause of death in either list."

"Four?" Tyler asked.

"What?"

"You said four people. His wife, Joe, Marc's mom. Who else?"

Candy looked at the carpet. Why did every single hotel have the same shitty tan carpet? "My dad died in a car accident last year. He was drunk at the time."

"Jesus, why didn't you tell us?" Tyler stood up. "Candy, I'd have come if you told me. Why would you keep something like that from me?"

"You were in the middle of recording and it wasn't that big a deal."

"Wasn't a big deal? Candy, it was your dad."

"Oh, God. I'm sorry I brought it up. Look, you brought me here to talk about Sandy." Suddenly, Candy could smell the wet greenery of the floral arrangements. The dim, cool room. Wood paneling, red carpet and matching drapes. Dozens of people coming around to tell her what a wonderful man her father was, completely unaware that she hadn't seen the man for years despite living in the same city. Helen flew in from California. Ronnie and Tanya had come from New York, where Ronnie was recording. Ricky had been in Australia on a shoot or he would have come, too. She hadn't told anyone else. Sandy held her hand and she sobbed. Not for her dad, but for Joe who had been more of a father to her and had been gone for less than a year. "Sandy doesn't want to abandon you, but he can't bear to see any of you destroy yourselves on his watch."

"We're not going to destroy ourselves," Marc grumbled.

"Odds are you will and even if you don't, it's not going to help you any. The road to fame and fortune is littered with the bodies of also-rans who crashed and burned. Tessa wrote a report on it for your reading pleasure."

"Great. Homework," Brian grumbled.

"It never ends. Personally, I don't care what you do."

"That's cold." Jason folded his arms.

"Then let me rephrase. If you destroy yourselves, I will cry at your funeral, but I don't feel it's my place to tell you one way or another. You're all big boys and you can make your own decisions. One of those decisions is the choice between the full rock star party and Sandy. And on that note, I'm going to go back to my room. I'm going to need a decision by tomorrow morning before ten because that's when I have to leave for my flight." She picked up her purse and started for the door.

"Candy, wait." Tyler grabbed her arm, pulling her into the hall. "Why didn't you tell me about your dad?"

"I told you. You were in the middle of recording the last album. I got the call early on a Wednesday and had him in the ground by Friday."

"You could have come to the studio and hung out with us at least."

"You were busy. It was fine. I don't know what you're so worried about it. It was months ago."

"I don't like to think of you alone through that." He stroked her arm.

Candy forced herself to ignore how good that felt. "I wasn't alone. Tessa and I went to New York for the weekend and hung out with Tanya and Ricky, and some of their friends. We were in *US Magazine*. I was mislabeled as their sister."

"Really?" Tyler looked a little gray.

"Yeah, they ran a picture of the three of us walking out of a club and captioned it Ronnie Bauer's children, Tanya, Candy, and Ricky. They ran a retraction the next week, but you know how that goes. Once something like that is out in the world, you can't retract it convincingly. And Ronnie loves to screw with people so he's saying something different every time somebody asks. I'm going to go back to my room. I have some work to do." Candy stepped away from him. "Let me know when you reach a decision."

"You know what we're going to decide." He trailed after her as she walked toward the elevators.

"Yeah, but let me live in suspense for at least an hour." She jabbed the call button. Maybe it would be better to take the stairs.

"Hey Candy! You still out there?" Brian leaned out of the room. "Great. You're still here. Want to have dinner?"

"Dinner?"

Brian strolled down the hall, grinning. "I can't stand these guys for another day. Help me, Candy, you're my only hope."

"Okay." Candy glanced at Tyler. If he'd noshed on a whole lemon, he'd have a cheerier expression. *What was he pissed off about now?* Not getting an invite to her dad's funeral? Like that had been fun. He couldn't be angry about the press calling her Ronnie Bauer's kid. He had always been jealous of the relationship she had with Ricky, being labeled as his sister could only be a good thing.

"Fantastic." Brian spun around to run back to the room.

Crap. In ten seconds she was going to be the entertainment at a band dinner. "Brian! Just you, okay? I don't want to deal with the whole three-ring circus." The elevator doors opened behind her. She stepped inside.

"Sure thing, you and me."

The doors closed in front of her. Double crap. Tyler probably thought she was excluding him. Maybe she should call and tell him he could come to dinner, too. But as fun as he'd been a few minutes ago, she'd rather not. Brian was fun and light and wouldn't come over all heavy on her because he didn't invite him to her father's funeral of all things.

* * * *

Tyler spotted Candy from halfway across the party. A second later, he registered Frankie and groaned. If he'd known this was going to happen he'd have skipped this event.

"What?" Marc asked. "Oh. She brought her new arm candy."

Tyler turned back. Candy looked amazing. Jeans, heels, yellow top, diamonds. He hadn't seen her in person since the Sandy thing eight months ago and she still looked like a million. All for Frankie who had decked out in expensively worn jeans and a wife-beater shirt. Make that, Candy had decked him out. He wasn't just her boyfriend, he was her client, and she was good at what she did. Very good. Which was why she was leading him over here right now, to make it look like he was running with the big dogs.

"Slimy little one-hit wonder," Marc muttered, hiding his comment by taking a sip from his glass. Then he put on the big smile. "Candy!"

"Hi, Tyler. Marc." Candy let go of Frankie to put her hands on his shoulders and kiss his cheek. Then she did the same to Marc. Did she linger a moment longer on his cheek than Marc's or was it wishful thinking? "You know Frankie."

"I've heard him. Nice tune." Marc shook Frankie's hand so Tyler did, too.

Frankie draped his arm over her shoulders. Bastard. Marc and Frankie started making small talk about Frankie's newest album that had dropped a couple of days ago. Candy listened politely. Tyler tried to pay attention to the conversation, but he was distracted by Candy. Did she look tired? Anxious? Unhappy? Had she looked like that last month when they were setting up the last details of the publicity for the new album?

"Tessa said Bear was going off radar in about a month." Candy leaned against Frankie. Didn't she know she was killing him?

"Taking a vacation before we start tour rehearsals. He's back home to pick up a car."

"We'll have to get together before Jason goes back to New York next week. He's got to bounce through a couple of local markets on the way to push the single."

"He's thrilled."

"You've got to go to New York?" Frankie asked.

"No, I've got to meet with the band before Jason goes back to New York. He's scheduled for the *Howard Stern Show* in two weeks." Candy stroked Frankie's arm.

"How come you can't get me on the *Howard Stern Show*?"

Marc caught his gaze and rolled his eyes.

"We've put together a great campaign for you."

"But I'm not on *Howard Stern*."

Candy gave him a blank look. Tyler knew that look too well. She wasn't going to argue. The discussion ended. After a second, she slid her arm through Frankie's. "I'll make it up to you."

Frankie stroked his fingers under her chin. "You better."

Tyler bit back a groan. Did they have to do this right here in front of him?

"I'll get you a drink." Frankie kissed her cheek.

"Thank you."

Frankie ambled off with that lucky-dumb-fuck look on his face that was getting him more magazine covers and airplay than he deserved.

"Still got it, don't you?" Marc asked her after he'd walked away.

"Got what?"

"The ability to turn men into obedient Jell-O."

"Fuck off," Candy said.

"What are you doing with that moron anyway?" Marc asked. "Is he that good in bed?"

"Actually, yes and sometimes that's all you need, isn't it?"

Tyler swallowed a ball of acid making its way up his throat. "When do you want to get together. Next week good for you?"

Chapter 7

Candy clicked the refresh button again. No doubt about it. She had no more work to distract her. Being in the same place with Tyler and Frankie was like a science experiment where you put one hand in a bowl of warm water and the other in a bowl of ice water, but instead of canceling each other out, it had created a violent storm front all along her nerves.

When she walked into the room, Frankie set aside his guitar and held out his hand. Just the two of them for once. She slid down next to him.

"All done?" Frankie asked, slipping his hand down her back and tucking it into the waistband of her jeans.

"For now. I sent out a bunch of emails trying to get you some late night appearances."

He laid her back on the couch, kissing her throat. "I love when you talk dirty."

"We should move this into the bedroom before we get too carried away."

He bit her shoulder. "You are such a smoking' babe I don't want to wait. I'll make it up to you later. And then again after that."

"Thank you."

He stretched out beside her. "I mean it. You are everything I ever wanted. Sweet and wonderful and sexy. And you taste fantastic." He bit her again and she moaned.

She reached for his pants wanting to feel him inside her. All day she'd been wound up wanting to be touched. Frankie pulled at her clothes as if he needed her as much as she needed him. He was never as gentle as Tyler. Why was she even thinking about Tyler now?

"Damn it." Frankie groped the end table. "Where are the fucking condoms?"

Candy batted his hand out of the way and pulled open the drawer. He sat up so she could rip it open and roll it on.

"I loved looking at you today, baby." He nuzzled her neck, thrusting into her hard. "You are so fucking hot."

"Yes. Harder." Candy sank her nails into his back, arching to draw him deeper into her. She squeezed her eyes closed. "It's wonderful. Wonderful. I was thinking about you too. Please, please." The tension wound tighter and tighter until it unraveled. "Oh, God, Tyler!"

Frankie stopped moving.

Candy held her breath. She hadn't said what she thought she'd said. She couldn't have. It was impossible.

"You called me Tyler." Frankie pulled away from her.

"It was an accident. I was with him all day and—"

"And what, Candy? You wanted to fuck him? You're thinking about him while I'm fucking you?"

"No, not at all." Panic clawed up her throat. "Please, Frankie. It was a mistake."

"You fucking whore." Frankie grabbed her arm, pulling her off the couch. Her knees banged against the floor sending shockwave of fear up her spine. "'I'm done with him. It's over.' But you jump whenever there's a chance to spend the day with him."

"They're my clients, too. Frankie, you're hurting me."

He threw her backward and she hit her head on the end table. For a second the whole world wavered.

"Goddamn you," Frankie snarled. He took a step forward, but when she cringed, he retreated. "You need to get out right fucking now."

"Frankie, it's one o'clock in the morning. Where am I supposed to go?"

"You think I care? Get the fuck out."

Candy scrambled to her feet, grabbing for her clothes. She dressed in the foyer and grabbed her purse. Her phone was in the front pocket. She scrolled through her contacts with trembling fingers until she found the one she needed. "Ronnie?"

"What's the matter, babe?" Of course Ronnie would be wide awake and alone at this hour.

"I—Frankie and I had a fight. Can I come to your place?"

"Of course. You coming now?"

"Yes."

"Are you okay to drive? You sound pretty shaken up. I can send someone to get you."

Candy dropped her keys trying to unlock her car. "No, I'm fine to drive. I'll be there in a little while." She hung up and dropped her phone in the cup holder. As she slid into the driver's seat, she glanced back at the door. No Frankie beckoning her back. She'd always known he was temporary, but he had been good in bed when he wasn't trying to mark his territory and he needed her too much to screw up. Frankie wasn't the best decision she'd ever made, but she'd never intended to hurt him. He'd probably be on the phone begging her to come back as soon as he cooled off. He was nothing without her.

The drive to Ronnie's house seemed to take an eternity. Her stomach was grinding on itself in time to the pounding in her head. Jorge was swinging the gates open as she turned into the driveway. When she drove up to the house, Ronnie was standing outside barefoot. He pulled her out of the car.

"Candy, my God, what happened? You're bleeding." He lifted her hair to look and the sharp pain made her gasp. "Did he hit you?"

"I fell into the end table." Candy shuddered. Frankie had a tough image, she'd put it together herself, but his sudden violence had been a surprise. She'd always thought he was more the type to storm away instead of lashing out.

That he was more like Tyler.

"You fell." Ronnie narrowed his eyes.

"I know how it sounds. Please, I don't want to talk about it."

"You need to see a doctor."

Candy shook her head and the world swam around her.

"I'll call someone. She can come out tonight. You need to be looked at. You might have a concussion." Ronnie glared at her. He wasn't going to accept anything short of total acquiescence.

"Doesn't matter. I won't sleep tonight anyway." Candy followed him into the house. The decorating bore the heavy stamp of Tanya, lush and spartan at the same time. "Where's your current woman?"

"I'm between right now, so there's no one to get in the way of this father-daughter chat we need to have about you and the men you choose."

"You're not my father."

"Convince the press of that. They're still looking for records." Ronnie picked up the phone and the person who answered also sounded wide-awake even though it was now approaching two AM.

Candy touched the back of her head and her fingers came away sticky. Her head did throb and she had hit it pretty hard. Everything burned, ached, and shook. If Tyler ever found out Frankie had grabbed her the way he had, he'd murder him.

"Alright, the doctor is on her way to take a look at you. Now, are you going to tell me what really happened or are you going to let me make it up on my own? I have a plentiful imagination, you know." He sat down on the couch and patted the seat beside him. "Come on now."

"I don't want to get blood on the couch."

"I can have it cleaned." He waved her over.

Candy sat down next to him and leaned her head on his shoulder. The comfort of the lean canceled out the pain of the motion. "It was nothing. We got into a fight. It got rough. I left."

"How rough?"

"Rough enough that I fell into an end table."

Ronnie pulled up the sleeve of her shirt. "Rough enough that you've got red marks on your arm about the size and shape of a man's hand."

Candy pulled her sleeve down. "Please, let's drop it, okay?"

"You should press charges."

"I don't want to press charges."

"And how are you going to feel when he hurts the next girl? The one who doesn't have anywhere to run or won't because she thinks he loves her."

"Ronnie, please. It won't happen like this with anyone else. No one can hurt him like I did."

"That doesn't excuse it."

"I know, but I can't deal with it right now. Believe me when I tell you nobody could bring violence out of him the way I did. He was always careful with me. He—tonight—it was a really bad fight."

Ronnie nodded. "Tanya will want to rip his balls off."

"I'm sure, but I'd rather avoid that. He wouldn't be a very popular soprano."

"I'm pretty sure Tyler will have something to say about it, too."

"Please, please don't tell him." Tears welled up in her eyes. Tyler would want to know what happened in excruciating detail and having to admit it would be like having her skin flayed off. She didn't need him knowing how much she missed him and how much she still wanted him. "Please Ronnie, promise me."

The bell rang.

"Saved by the bell." Ronnie stood up and got the door.

Candy closed her eyes. No one could have hurt Frankie the way she had. She'd never called anyone that before. Why tonight? Why ever? How could she have?

* * * *

Tyler leaned back in the booth not sure if he wished he were anywhere but here or was really fucking glad to witness this firsthand.

Marc had called about two hours ago saying he was at the Whisky with Trent and Gian from SendDown, where they met up with Frankie, who was a complete mess because he and Candy had broken up. Marc hadn't been able to figure out who broke up with who, but it hadn't been a mutual decision. Frankie kept saying he threw her out, but considering how deep he was in the bottle, Marc doubted it.

So Tyler had come out to watch the circus.

Trent, who had always had aspirations toward Candy, kept feeding Frankie drinks and pumping him for information, most of which Tyler didn't want to hear. He already knew what a great lover she was and how wonderful she was. He didn't need the blow by blow from her most recent wreckage.

Ronnie Bauer walked in and automatically he and Marc straightened up. Gian went rigid. Trent tried to act as if he wasn't impressed, and failed.

"Hello, boys." Ronnie glanced around the table. "Frankie, can I have a moment?"

Frankie blinked at him blearily. He pushed himself to his feet and followed Ronnie a few feet away where he leaned in to listen to Ronnie talk, his face getting whiter and whiter by the second. At one point he asked something and Ronnie gave his head a decisive shake.

"What's going on?" Gian asked.

"Bauer thinks of Candy like a daughter. Looks like he doesn't like the way it went down. I bet Frankie is telling the truth when he says he threw her out and she went straight to Ronnie."

Not like she'd come to his house. Tyler leaned forward to watch.

The faint smile had never left Ronnie's mouth and never reached his eyes. Frankie's face faded from white to gray.

"Whatever he's saying, it must be good." Marc leaned across the table and moved his lips as if he was trying to copy Ronnie's.

"If my daughter shows up on my doorstep late at night after breaking up with her boyfriend, I'm probably not going to be friendly either." Tyler took a deep draft of his beer. What could have happened that would bring Bauer down here like this? He wasn't here to have a quiet drink with his not-daughter's most recent ex. The whole vibe felt less like family business and more like mafia business. Bauer had always been more of a friendly uncle than the Godfather had, but the way he looked tonight was different. Menacing. What had Frankie done to bring out Bauer's dark side? Tyler didn't like where his imagination was going. Not with Candy in the picture.

Ronnie took a step back from Frankie and nodded sharply. Tyler was pretty sure he read lips well enough to pick up a "got it?" before Ronnie turned away.

Tyler shoved away from the table intent on chasing down Ronnie. If nothing else, he needed to know Candy was okay. As he rushed past, Frankie was puking on the floor.

"Ronnie! Ronnie, wait!"

Ronnie stopped and turned around, smiling with his whole expression.

Tyler felt a bit like a favored son. "What was that all about?" he asked.

"Candy was in a state when she got to my house last night and she hasn't been herself all day. I wanted to have a chat with Frankie about it, just to put him straight."

"Is she all right?"

"She'll be fine."

"What happened?"

Ronnie put a hand on his shoulder. "I promised her I wouldn't say, but I wanted to make sure nothing like it ever happens again. Candy is fine, but she's selling the house she was living with him in. She'll be at my house until she decides to find a place of her own again if you'd like to come over. I think it would be good for her to see you."

Good for her to see him? "Why?"

Ronnie shook his head. "She's upset. Might be good for her to know you still care about her."

Tyler blanched. Was he that obvious?

Ronnie laughed. "You think I'm blind? I see the way you look at her and I had a one true love once. Give her a call tomorrow and see if she's up for a visit. But do me a favor and don't tell her I was here tonight."

"Sure."

"See you later."

Tyler stared after Ronnie. He hadn't stayed for a drink. Just long enough to traumatize Frankie and invite Tyler to his house to check on Candy. When Tyler returned to the table, Frankie was gone. "Where'd he go?"

Trent laughed. "Ronnie Bauer told Frankie he was going to wreck his fucking life if he didn't stay away from Candy. If anything happens that he doesn't like, Frankie's going to be flipping burgers for the rest of his life. I didn't know the old man had balls like that."

"He doesn't need balls." Marc stared meaningfully at Tyler. "He's got power."

* * * *

Candy's head still throbbed though the doctor didn't think it was a concussion. Her arm hurt too, but no worse than her heart. She had liked Frankie and had never wanted to hurt him. If she'd accidentally called him Brian, he'd have laughed it off, but to call him Tyler? She answered her phone without looking.

"Hi Candy."

Speak of the devil. "Yes, Tyler."

"I heard what happened. Are you okay?"

Candy gritted her teeth, which made her head hurt worse. "I'm fine."

"Are you sure? How about I come to see?"

"How did you even find out?"

"Marc was down at the Whisky last night and ran into Frankie drowning his sorrows."

"Small world." Poor Frankie. If he was only one of her clients, she'd have recommended he do more public sorrow drowning because it played into his image, but personally she hated the fact that she'd been the cause of it.

"Candy."

"Listen, I'm fine. I'm fine. Everything is just dandy." Candy leaned back from the computer.

Ronnie was noodling on the piano in the other room. He was supposed to be in the studio, but he'd cancelled to stay around the house with her. He'd gone out for a bit last night, but hadn't been gone long and she suspected he'd been smoking because he came back smelling of cigarettes. Old habits died hard.

Ricky was flying in from London and Tanya would be coming from Milan as soon as she could get away. As much as they weren't her family, they were her family.

"I'd feel better to see for myself." Tyler folded his arms. Speaking of family. If Tyler and Marc had been at the Whisky, all of them knew, too. Sandy was going to be on the phone soon enough. He would require a visit, too. It was like calling hours at an extremely exclusive funeral home. Ronnie Bauer's Heartbreak Home specializing in months-long calling hours for an exclusive few.

"I'm staying with Ronnie. I couldn't be safer at the White House."

"I figured."

"Why would you figure that?" Why would he make the leap that she was staying with Ronnie? It was just as likely that she went to a hotel or to one of her other friend's.

"I...assumed. I mean, if I had an open invitation to stay with Ronnie Bauer, that's where I'd go. Right?"

He was still the worst liar in the world. "You're busy. You don't have to take time out of your day to come here to check on me."

"Until we start rehearsal, I have the time."

He was also relentless. All she had to do was keep it together for a couple of hours. "Fine. You know the way to Ronnie's. I have a couple of meetings this afternoon and one tomorrow morning."

"I'll see you tomorrow afternoon then."

Good, twenty-four more hours for the bruises to fade and the headache to go away. "I'll see you tomorrow."

* * * *

Candy opened the door and spread her arms. "See. Perfectly fine."

"Don't be a bitch, Candy. I was worried about you."

"You and everybody else. I've been on the phone nonstop."

"Word got around. Frankie was pretty broken up the other night. And last night, from what I hear. Possibly into this morning if Trent can be trusted."

"I thought you said Marc ran into Frankie." Candy folded her arms. The sleeve of her shirt tightened around her bruised arm. It had become a beautiful array of purples.

Tyler shuffled. "He did. Then he called me and I went out to join them. Trent and Gian were there too."

"Why, so you could adjourn the first meeting of the We Hate Candy fan club?"

"Nobody hates you, Candy."

"Why don't we go out back and have a drink?" Candy led him to the patio where Ronnie was fiddling on his computer.

"Hey, you're here. Drink?" He put aside the computer. "Candy, Coke?"

"Thank you."

"Tyler?"

"Gin and tonic if you've got it."

Ronnie headed for the bar as Candy hung back for a moment. Tyler looked good. Tanned and comfortable. Frankie had always been nervous around Ronnie. "The album is doing well," Ronnie said from the bar. "Nice change after that last one."

"Tell me about it. I thought the magic was gone and I was going to have to go back to construction work." Tyler sat down.

Candy laughed. Construction work. With multi-platinum albums behind them and Sandy watching their money all these years, any of the guys in Touchstone could quit and do whatever the hell they wanted.

"Nah, you keep making music whether it sells or not. Eventually the public will catch up."

"Are you on your third or fourth panned album?"

"Third, but who's counting, you young whippersnapper?"

Candy stretched her shoulders and her sleeves slipped up her arms. She really needed to look for her own place to live. She couldn't freeload off Ronnie forever, but the thought of being alone creeped her out a little. It was nice to sit around and have normal conversations with friends.

"What the fuck is that?" Tyler demanded. He reached for her elbow, turning her arm to inspect the bruise. "Frankie do it?"

Or not. "Tyler drop it." She tried to twist her arm away from him but couldn't escape. He wasn't using any pressure, but he had her firmly caught.

"I'm not going to drop it. What else did he do to you? I'm going to break his fucking neck."

"I left. Isn't that enough for the two of you? He was never violent before."

"Really? Because you have a history of forgiving assholes."

"Says the ex."

Tyler flushed. "I was talking about your dad."

"Your dad?" Ronnie demanded. "The dad we buried?"

"You were at the funeral?" Tyler asked. "You didn't have time to get in touch with me, but you could call him?"

Ronnie ignored him. "Candy, what's this about your dad? Did he beat you or something?"

"It was a long time ago." Candy slouched into a chair forcing Tyler to release her.

"Ronnie said it was bad, but Candy—"

"Ronnie said?" Candy straightened. None of the pieces of this puzzle fit together as they were telling her it did. "What do you mean Ronnie said?"

Ronnie jerked. "I picked up the phone when he called yesterday."

But at the same time Tyler said, "The night before last."

"The night before last? What happened the night before last?" She glared at Ronnie. "I told you to stay out of it."

"No, you told me not to tell him." Ronnie pointed at Tyler.

"So you went and talked to Frankie in front of him instead?"

Ronnie leaned on the table scowling. "You called me at quarter after one crying and saying you needed someplace to go. You turned up at my door half an hour later bleeding."

"Bleeding?" Tyler asked. "What do you mean bleeding?"

"You can't expect me to do nothing." Ronnie continued as if Tyler hadn't spoken. "Nobody does something like that to one of mine and gets away with it. Nobody does that to a little girl and gets away with it where I can stop it."

"What did you do?" Candy stood, leaning into his face. "What did you do to Frankie?"

"What do you mean, bleeding?" Tyler stood too. "Candy."

"Nothing. Yet. You said you wouldn't press charges so I made other plans."

"What other plans?" Candy shouted.

"I told him if he ever touched you again or if I ever heard he'd raised a hand to another woman, I would ruin him."

"Ruin him?" Candy caught her breath. Ronnie could do it. He'd made Touchstone. He could ruin a career as easily and Frankie's career was in its infancy.

"I told him I would buy his contract just to break it and I'd make sure no other record company would pick him up. He would never record another note or show up on another short-lived sitcom as long as he lived. Believe you me, Tanya will make sure my wishes are carried out in the event of my death. If you'd let me, I'd destroy him now."

Distantly, Candy heard Tyler catch his breath. Her head pounded again. She wasn't sure if what he'd done pleased or horrified her. Putting her hand over her mouth, Candy sat back down. Ronnie and Tyler stood on either side of the table staring at her. "It was a mistake. I made a mistake and it all went out of control."

Ronnie sat down beside her and took her hands in his. "Candy, I know you wanted to let it lie, but I couldn't. When you got out of the car the other night, I wanted to go to his house and bash his fucking face in. He crossed a line, sweetheart. I had to shove him back over."

Candy glanced at Tyler. He was still standing and looked pissed. She turned back to Ronnie. What was done was done and no matter how she felt about it, she couldn't change it. Besides, Ronnie did it out of a misguided desire to protect her. How could she fault him? She nodded.

"I want to know what happened and I want to know right fucking now," Tyler snarled.

"Sit down, please." She used the moment that took him to take a deep breath. Yesterday she'd thought she could keep it together for a couple of hours and she'd managed all of fifteen minutes. "Frankie and I had a fight. Things were said and he grabbed my arm. I pulled away and fell into the end table, cutting my head. I called Ronnie to ask if I could come here. I didn't know I was bleeding until I got here, but it was from hitting my head. You know how head wounds bleed."

"He's not working with Jerry again, I promise you that." Tyler dug in his pocket.

"Don't. Let it go."

"Candy, I'm not going to let some bully go around beating up girls. I sic security on guys who are rough at shows. I'm not going to stand around with my thumb up my ass while some jackass beats you up again."

"It was an argument between a couple. It has nothing to do with you."

"It does too!"

Candy slammed her hand on the table. "I can take care of myself."

"By running to Ronnie."

"Who was I supposed to run to? You? I probably would have interrupted you with your current mattress."

Tyler pursed his lips.

"Okay, enough." Ronnie stood up and put his hands between them. "We don't need to make this personal. Candy, we want to protect you. You protect us. You've been fretting for two days about Jason."

"What about Jason?" Tyler still looked pissed, but she could see the distraction from the subject change in his eyes. He'd never been good at hanging onto things, topics of conversation, grudges, women.

Candy sunk back into her chair. Damn Ronnie. He knew where to catch her every time. "I've gotten conflicting calls from some of my sources. That he's shopping for other women and for rings and that Stella has been getting cozy with a couple of B-listers. They're either breaking up or getting hitched and nobody wants either."

"One way or the other, he's going to be a total asshole on tour." Tyler had sat down, too. For a minute, she'd been deluded into thinking he cared for her as more than a friend. No, he'd made his choice years ago, and it hadn't been her.

* * * *

Tyler sat at the conference table waiting. The sooner this meeting ended, the better. He had his assignments.

"Jason, how are things with Stella?"

"Fine." Jason gave her a blank look, which absolutely meant he was up to something.

"I can't do my job if you aren't straight with me."

"I'm straight with you. Things are fine."

Candy put her fists on her hips, glaring at him.

"What about you, Candy?" Bear asked. "You still living at Ronnie's?"
"I'm fine."

"Great." Bear stood and put his hands flat on the table. "Now that we've determined everyone is fine, we can go."

"Don't be a dick, Bear," Brian muttered, picking at his calluses.

Bear sat back down.

"No, he's right. We're done here." Candy shook her head, shuffling papers into her briefcase. "Everybody remember to smile, smile, smile. The last album was great. This album is greater. Yada yada. Jason, wear a watch so you don't miss your flights. You know radio gofers don't get paid enough to keep track of the time."

"Yep." Jason strolled out, whistling.

"He's up to something," Candy grumbled. "Brian, what is he up to?"

"How should I know?"

Marc laughed.

"Shut up. It's not like we show up in matching outfits."

"Anymore." Marc rolled his eyes toward Brian.

"That was so cute." Bear pouted. "Why did you ever stop?"

"Fuck off." Brian looked at his watch. "I have to get home."

"Yeah, I'm sure Bonnie had some really important shopping she needs to get done."

Brian walked out. Candy scooped up her bag and followed him, hopefully, only going down the hall to Tessa's office. After sitting through that whole boring meeting, he didn't want to lose her now. Bear and Marc stared at him. Naturally, today the band hung around after the meeting. Most times they had these little gatherings he expected them to all get stuck in the door trying to get out.

"What?" Tyler asked.

"What are you waiting for?" Marc leaned forward.

"Nothing. What are you waiting for?"

Marc arched an eyebrow. "We see."

"You see what?"

"Come on." Bear stood up. "I don't want to hang around here too long or Sandy will come up with a reason to lecture us about something. Tony sent me pictures of the Plymouth Satellite he found. It's a '72. It's gonna be sweet when I get done with it."

Tyler followed them out of the room trying to look interested in Bear's newest car, but he couldn't summon the will. Bear had about six of them now and he only drove the two.

"… hate it when he gets sneaky," Tessa was saying as he passed her office. "It's always a flaming disaster."

That seemed like a plausible opening to duck in on.

Tessa knelt on the floor surrounded by piles of paper. "How is it that we have to spend so much time mopping up their love lives?"

Candy leaned on the wall inside the door. "Tell me about it. I went to law school for this. You need something, Tyler?"

"No, just didn't have any place else to be right away and I'm going to get to hear all about Bear's car on tour." He smiled at them trying to look harmless and bored. Five minutes with Candy and he could convince her to go to dinner with him. Over dinner, he could lay the groundwork on his new master plan.

She'd just broken up with Frankie so she wouldn't be looking for anything permanent right away. Besides, he was going on tour, so he wasn't looking to start anything until after anyway.

They could take it easy, keep it quiet, and after the tour maybe explore getting back together. Sounded like a perfectly good plan. Didn't it?

"Well, I'll see you. Call me if you hear anything." Candy straightened from the wall and stretched.

They must have been talking while he stood there daydreaming about getting back together with her. He followed her down the hall. When they passed Helen's open office door, Candy waved. "So you wanna catch some lunch or something?" he asked.

"Dinner."

"Yeah." He looked at his wrist before he remembered he never wore a watch. "It's time to eat, isn't it? Or do you have more meetings today?"

"No, I'm clear after this. Why do you want to have dinner?"

"Just to talk. Is there something wrong with that?"

"I guess not. Hi, Jody."

"What is going on with Jason?" Jody demanded from behind the reception desk.

Candy smirked at her.

"It's not like that." But Jody went instantly red. "I'm trying to put together the blog and if there's news, I need it. How much can I write about Bear's new car? It's a car for Christ sake. He's already got like ten of them."

"But it's something the fans may be interested in. And don't forget to thank everyone who sent presents to Brian's son for his birthday. The poor kid is going to drown in stuffed animals." Candy reminded her.

"Brian said they were going to put them into a room like a ball pit." Tyler tapped on the reception desk.

"Don't put that in the blog." Candy adjusted her jacket over her shoulders.

"I'm not an idiot." Jody rolled her eyes. "What is going on with Jason?"

"I'm trying to find that out myself. He's being sneaky again."

"I hate that."

"Everybody does."

"Where are you two going?"

Candy glanced back at Tyler, but he couldn't read her expression to tell how she felt about being paired with him again. "Apparently we're going to dinner because we're old friends. Are you going to put that in the blog?"

Tyler wondered if he was blushing now. He should have called her at home, or better, gone over to her house and ambushed her there. No, she was staying at Ronnie's, and Ronnie, Ricky and Tanya were all there. He'd have been the one ambushed.

"You're hilarious. Have fun and tell me as soon as you know anything about Jason."

"Pinky swear." Candy pushed out the doors. "Your car or mine?"

"I'll drive." This was too easy. It was going to come unglued. It had to.

"You know, we could skip dinner and go to your place." She gave in a sweet, sly smile and for a second they were kids again in her father's house as she led him down the hall to her bedroom for the first time. "Nah, I'm starved. Take me to dinner."

* * * *

Inside the door, he let go of her long enough to lock it. When he turned back, she was standing there with her arms behind her, thrusting her breasts forward. She looked damned adorable and incredibly sexy. He pressed her against the closed door, kissing her. The way she tasted. The way her eyes shone. Why had he ever left her? She wrapped her arms around his neck pulling herself up his body. Tyler shuddered. "I miss you. I miss you more than I've ever missed anyone."

"Tyler," she murmured. "Let's go to bed."

Dinner had been really nice. Really, really nice. He'd never gotten to lay out his master plan, but it didn't matter. For the first time in years, she was talking to him as someone she liked instead of someone she tolerated. It was beautiful. Like getting back into Eden after camping at the gates for decades.

And now she was in his house leading him down the hall to his bedroom. Hell, why wait until after the tour? Groupies were boring. They all wanted to make him feel better, but they had an extremely limited bag of tricks.

She cupped his cheek and kissed him. The heavy link between them wrapping around him like a blanket on a cold day. He took a breath, drawing it down to his soul. He laid her on her back, letting his hand run down her side. Candy arched, smiling at him. "Just like old times."

"I like old times."

"You do?"

"I like them way better than I like the new times." He traced her lower lip. "Remember back when we were together, you would look at me across the room and I could tell by the look on your face I was the only one in the room for you?"

She put her hands on his cheeks. They were so warm and real. "You were the only one in the room for me."

He kissed her. When he touched her warm lips, she closed her eyes. Every moment she spent with him, she made him feel like the center of the universe. The whole time they'd been apart, he'd felt half there. Now, the desperate longing to be with her every second nearly destroyed him. What was he going to do on tour?

Candy straightened and pulled her shirt off. "I want you."

"You're a bad girl."

"But in all the right places."

He crawled over her. The heady, flowery scent of her heated skin made him crazy. He'd forgotten the amazing scent coming from her. Delicious. It made his skin ache and tingle. He trailed kisses down her neck and between her breasts. "You're such a lovely girl."

"I thought I was a bad girl."

"You're a lovely bad girl." He traced one of her nipples with the tip of his tongue.

She gasped, arching.

"I missed you," he murmured

Writhing, she moaned. "That feels so good."

He trailed further down her body searching for all those remembered places. She had been his first and no one had ever measured up.

"The way your mouth feels..." Her words were lost in a pleasured sigh as he licked the crease at the top of her thigh. "Oh, Tyler." Candy dug her fingers into the sheets as he spread her legs. Her muscles shivered like overstrung rubber bands. He ran his fingers up the back of her thigh to her knee and stayed there, nestled in the crook behind her knee without moving. She was glorious. Staring at her laying on his bed, he realized she was his first in more ways than sex. She believed in him, challenged him, fought for him. If only he could tell her how much she meant to him.

Trying to articulate a thought took too much effort. She opened her eyes and he thought he saw understanding in them. Like she wanted to say so much, but couldn't. Then she held out her arms.

Smiling, he stretched out on top of her, angling his leg under hers to spread her wider open. She moaned, burying her hands in his hair as he kissed her. Nothing was like this. Nothing had ever been like this. She wrapped her legs around his hips. "Please, please." She whimpered.

He started riding against her. Through his jeans, his cock strained for her. "This works better without pants."

She laughed breathlessly.

He got back up on his knees and pulled off his shirt before reaching for his jeans. "I planned to tease you a little more. I underestimated you." He pushed down his jeans and fell on her, thrusting.

When he buried himself in her, Candy cried out. He lost himself to the endless rhythm of their bodies moving together. Distantly, he heard delighted cries. It could always be like this. Open. Wide open and vulnerable. Ecstasy gathered in him and uncoiled. Candy's arms tightened around him as her body shuddered with his.

It could always be like this. Forever.

Chapter 8

Candy opened her eyes. The ceiling was painted a pale, soothing blue. She had found the house and had it decorated for Tyler while he was on tour. All he'd had to do was walk through the front door and unpack his suitcase.

Rebound sex with a previous ex. This had to be the dumbest stunt ever perpetrated by a woman. She could already hear Tessa and Tanya berating her for her amazing stupidity. She was going to suffer for this. Not because of Tyler. The man hadn't invented the term casual sex, but he had certainly taken it to heart. No, she was going to suffer the slings and arrows of fantasy, late at night remembering how good the relationship had been back then and how good the sex had been tonight.

Candy disentangled herself from Tyler who was still sound asleep. They'd ended up upside down on the bed. As generous and athletic as Tyler was, she was a little surprised they weren't hanging from the ceiling. She hobbled to the bathroom and searched for aspirin before she even looked in the mirror. Yeah, it had been unwise.

It had been just like old times. She'd always been able to talk to him and trust him, within his limits. He was a best friend she could have sex with, and he was a wonderful lover. Always gentle and attentive.

But he was her ex and her client and a whole swampy mess of emotional baggage she couldn't afford to unpack, ever. She had to get back to the Touchstone office and collect her car before anybody else got there. If it was still there when any of the office staff got in, she'd be neck deep in overbearing concern. First Sandy's office, then Tessa's, a brief stop at Helen's door where Helen would talk about anything and everything but

Tyler while expressing her deep concern for Candy's sanity with her eyes, and finally a grilling from Jody.

She had a meeting at ten she couldn't afford to show up for groggy. Glinda Dare was set to become the next super-starlet and they were meeting with Tanya at her boutique to go through potential outfits for the junket for her summer movie. Candy stepped into the shower.

"You didn't wake me." Tyler climbed in behind her, and wrapped his arms around her waist.

"I thought you might be tired." She scrubbed the washcloth over her face trying to remove the smeared make up. What a disaster. Her skin was going to be screwed up for days from sleeping with makeup on. She'd have to call Tori to see if she could get in for an emergency facial. "I need to get to the office to pick up my car. I have an appointment this morning and I need to go home and change."

"After we get out of the shower." Tyler nuzzled her neck. "It's not even seven yet. What time is your appointment?"

"Ten, but I have to go home and change."

"You've got time, relax."

"Tyler, don't." Candy pulled his arms apart so she could escape him. "Do you know what I did with my phone?"

"Pretty sure you left it in the car. We were kinda busy when we got in last night." He grinned, following her out of the shower.

Candy pulled on her blouse. Ronnie would notice that she hadn't come home last night. So would Tanya and Ricky. Damn, Jorge was probably going to be giving her side eye when he opened the gate. "Yes, we were. And it was fun, but I really have to get to work. I have a lot of irons in the fire." That wasn't true. She'd been flinging all of Frankie's stuff straight to him until he got a new publicist. Touchstone's campaign was set in stone. SendDown was on tour so all their stuff was either done or damn near. Glinda was ahead of the curve looking for junket outfits before her film got out of post. None of her other acting clients were there yet. Technically Ronnie was her client, but he hardly required any attention.

"Fun?" Tyler frowned.

He must not be used to being regarded as fun. The physical reaction was obvious since he was still naked from the shower.

"Yeah. You were always great in the sack and you've learned a lot since we were in high school." He better have, with all the tutors he'd had. Candy jammed her leg into her pants and heard a seam rip. Better and better. Pulling on her blouse more carefully, she settled it on her shoulders before buttoning it up. "Are you gonna get dressed so you can drive me to the office so I can get my car or should I call a cab?"

"I'll drive you." He opened a dresser drawer and pulled out a t-shirt, which he yanked on while locating underwear and jeans. "Ready when you are."

"Look, I want to thank you for last night." Candy started for the garage. "I really needed to get Frankie out of my system."

"Frankie?"

"I'm getting a little older and it was nice to have a younger man like him around. It stung getting dumped by him."

"He threw you into an end table."

"True, but it was nice to have a younger man attracted to me, and now he isn't." She pulled open the car door. Her bag was spilled all over the passenger-side floor. Her phone showed a message from her assistant, Sarina and forty-seven missed calls. Crap. She was only out of touch for a couple of hours. What could have happened in a couple of hours? The universe was punishing her for hooking up with Tyler. She opened Sarina's message.

Stella dumped Jason in People.

Candy's gut clenched. Her own little disgrace shrank to a pinpoint on the horizon in the face of this oncoming train. "Stella dumped Jason in *People*."

"What?" Tyler was already in the driver's seat starting the car.

"Stella dumped Jason in *People*. We need to stop at the nearest drug store so I can get a copy of *People* magazine."

"Don't you have that delivered to your office?"

"I need one now." Candy called her assistant. "Sarina, what's going on?"

"*People* has a spread on celebrity couples. Stella and Jason are in a sidebar titled So Over."

"Oh no. How are they even considered a celebrity couple? She's not a celebrity. She's barely a model."

"The phone has been going bananas since yesterday afternoon when it started showing up in people's mailboxes, but I couldn't get hold of you."

"I was busy." Busy screwing my ex-boyfriend. Genius. "It's a little late to do much in the way of damage control. You haven't heard from Jason?"

"He did the interview in Phoenix and the one in Atlanta and he sounded good."

"But he's got Howard Stern tomorrow."

"I know."

"But does he?"

"Anybody's ballgame."

"Super."

Tyler pulled into a CVS and parked. "You wait in the car. I'll go get the magazine."

Candy could have kissed him. "Okay, have you tried to get Jason?"

"No answer. Not on his cell and not at the New York apartment, but he's there. I called that liquor store in his neighborhood and they made a delivery to him late last night."

"Awesome. Book me a flight to New York as soon as possible. Do you think you can handle Glinda?"

"Handle Glinda?" Candy imagined Sarina going pale through the phone.

"Yes, handle Glinda. Meet her at Tanya's boutique on Rodeo and tell her I had an emergency and had to go to New York to make sure a client didn't go on national radio drunk."

"But what am I supposed to do?"

"Make sure Glinda doesn't end up wearing something Joan Rivers can get catty about. Either that or make sure she ends up in something so outrageous Joan Rivers will have no choice but to get catty about, whatever you're feeling at the moment."

"But Candy—"

"You have great taste and good instincts. She's in a superhero movie so it could go either way. Make sure she knows if she goes wild, she needs to be able to sell it. If she goes on national television wearing fishnet stockings and an embroidered handkerchief and isn't feeling it, she'll be a laughing stock. If she is, everybody will talk about how liberated she is. And Amanda will be there to help. Whatever Glinda tries on, watch her body language."

Tyler climbed back into the car and handed her the magazine open to the side bar. A photo of Jason and Stella walking hand-in-hand had been artfully torn.

"And I need you to call Sam at *People*. He should have warned me this was coming."

"I can do that."

"You can do all of it. Now get on it. Call me back with my flight information." Candy hung up still studying the picture. Unbe-freakin'-lievable. No wonder she'd been getting calls. "This is a disaster."

"Tell me about it. You don't have to be trapped on a bus with him all summer long."

"I shouldn't have been out of the loop all afternoon, yesterday."

"You can't be on call all the time."

"But Jason is probably devastated. He really seemed to like Stella, though God knows why. The woman was a harpy." She reached for her phone still staring at the magazine. "Maybe Sandy knows something. Or Tessa."

"Can you do that in a minute?" Tyler plucked her phone out of her fingers. "I need to talk to you."

"Let me call Tessa first."

"I need to talk to you about last night."

"It was just sex. What's there to talk about? I have a crisis to handle right now."

"Can you stop worrying about Jason for five fucking minutes?" Tyler shouted.

Candy frowned. "What is wrong with you? Don't worry about me making more out of last night than it was. I know how you feel about serious relationships and I'm not trying to force the issue, am I? It's not like you haven't made yourself clear."

"What do you mean?"

"Tyler, the last time you had any kind of serious relationship was with me and we broke up because it was too serious for you. Since then you've dated or lived with two dozen women and had sex with legions more."

"Not legions." Tyler turned into the parking lot. Her car was the only one there.

"Whatever. You have never had a relationship last more than three months. I get it. You don't want to be tied down. I got over it a long time ago." *I hope.* Otherwise, as soon as this thing with Jason was under control, she was going to be getting her own deliveries from the liquor store, which would get Ronnie involved again because he had way too many friends in AA and NA. She'd have to hear the story of the night he was at a party at Paul McCartney's house with Keith Moon when Keith said he wanted to go home because he wasn't feeling well and died. Good times.

"Candy—"

Candy put her finger over his lips. "You have a soft heart. I know. I really do. You don't want me to be hurt. I'm trying to tell you, I'm not. I really needed a vigorous shag to get Frankie out of my system and you did that, but I don't expect anything more out of you. Thank you." She kissed him and when she leaned away he looked dazed. Probably relief. "I've got to go. There's this fire I need to put out. I'll call you when I get back in town. Okay? Damn, I'm starving and there's no time to grab breakfast."

She hopped out of the car. On the way to her own her phone started ringing. At least she had something to distract her from her personal mess. "Hello Sarina, what's going on?"

* * * *

Tyler watched her walk across the parking lot, talking on the phone, not sure if he should be devastated that she was walking away or relieved. He was sort of trapped in the demilitarized zone between Hail Mary land and What-the-fuck-atania.

She was everything he ever wanted in a woman. Smart, fun, serious, capable, strong.

She was more than he needed. Demanding, overbearing.

Hot. That went both ways. She'd always been hot, but now she'd added numbers to her thermostat.

If she got her way, she'd be the first woman he ever fucked and the last. Groupies might be boring, but they were more plentiful than McDonald's. If the last one didn't satisfy, there would be another one around the corner.

Maybe this thing with Jason was a sign. Jason had been pretty serious about Stella all through the last tour. At the time it had meant more for the rest of them. Now it looked as if he'd wasted a lot of emotion on a woman who walked away from him.

If he got serious like that with Candy again, and she walked away, the results could be devastating. She was their publicist, which meant the band would be pissed at him. Add to that, she was in tight with Ronnie— the one who ultimately held their recording contract—who was out there playing her enforcer.

Tyler felt himself drifting toward Hail Mary land. Candy was too hot to handle. She wanted, needed, and demanded way too much and the cost of disappointing her was too high. He put the car in gear wondering if any of the bars on Sunset served breakfast. He needed to get together a party and the sooner the better.

* * * *

"Aren't you Tyler Franklin?"

Tyler looked up from his glass. The party he needed hadn't materialized. Probably because he'd spent all day sulking at home and fielding calls from everybody else wanting to gossip about Jason. It had helped to keep him from thinking about Candy. A couple of girls made their way by his secluded booth, but he couldn't summon the interest to even be charming enough to keep them around.

This guy didn't seem to need him to be charming or even paying attention. He slid into the booth. "Awesome. Did you come to see us play?"

Tyler studied the man. He could hear Candy's analysis in the back of his head. His blond hair was dry and weedy and needed shaping. He was wretchedly thin and needed a trainer or he'd never have the stamina to get through a tour. Skin care, clothes. He had the attitude though. This guy was exactly Candy's type. Maybe he should introduce them.

"I'm Brett Cherney. What did you think of the show?"

Where his booth was situated, he hadn't seen a thing. The audience liked it though. "You sounded great."

"Wow, thanks. That means a lot. We've had some interest from a couple of labels."

"Good. Make sure you get a good lawyer."

"Anybody you can recommend?"

"Call our office and talk to Tessa. See if she'll do some freelance."

"Tessa, right." Brett wrote the name on his hand. "You want another drink or something?" He stood up and waved. "Hey! Duke! Over here!"

Super, he was going to get that party whether he wanted it or not.

A dark-haired guy came over with a drink and sat down. "Nice find. Good to meet you."

Tyler looked at him. He knew what Candy would say about him too. "Women suck."

"No argument there." Duke reared back, shaking his head. He and Brett exchanged a look. "You know what the cure for that is."

"More women." Brett grinned.

* * * *

Tanya curled up on the couch bathed in the blinking lights of the Christmas tree. "Okay, you need to start at the top because this is like the world's most fabulous soap opera and this past year's episodes were excellent."

"Very funny. You're not living it." Candy combed knots out of the throw's fringe with her fingers.

"Dad said you were bleeding when you showed up here." Ricky was sitting on the floor in jeans and no shirt. He was such a good-looking guy. Why couldn't she fall for him? Nice, attractive, serially monogamous.

"I swear we got into a fight and I tripped into the end table. You know how head wounds bleed."

"The guy's a prick."

"It's not like I'm going to argue."

"Exactly, so drop it." Tanya shoved aside her teacup. "And what about Jason and Stella? I always hated her. She told me I needed to use her for my shows and I told her she needed to get a personality implant. She actually dumped him in *People*?"

"He said he had no idea it was coming. He picked up the magazine on his flight from Atlanta to New York. He expected to see her there. Fortunately, he managed to get a win out of Stern with it."

"He was very cool about the whole thing." Ricky studied the ice melting in his glass. "I loved the comment about switching from wire hangers to something with more shape."

"No more wire hangers," Tanya quoted.

Candy laughed. "That *was* genius. But he was such a total asshole all through the tour that they're thinking about shipping him off someplace to get his head together. Sandy's cousin stayed at some campground in West Virginia. The cabins are supposed to be nice and it should keep him out of trouble."

"This is Jason." Tanya smirked.

"I heard Bear punched him." Ricky rested his chin on his fist.

"I thought Bear poured a Coke over his head and Tyler punched him. Either way he really was being an asshole and probably deserved it."

"And what happened with Bear?"

"He met this school teacher while he was visiting home and almost made her lose her job on some kind of morality thing."

"Teachers can be fired on morality grounds?" Ricky asked. "That sounds so eighteenth century."

"I don't know. According to Maureen, they weren't trying to get her on morality, but that was behind it. They didn't like her dating a rock star. The lawsuit drags on. They're getting married next summer."

"That's so sweet. What about Marc?"

"Marc had no really significant issues this year. He's like a duck. Everything rolls off his back."

"Is Brian still married to his harpy?"

"I don't know what is going on in Brian's head. He always said he wanted to play the field forever, but he married Bonnie at the drop of a hat."

"She was pregnant," Tanya pointed out.

"Like that mattered. They could have shared custody. He didn't need to marry her and he doesn't need to stay married to her. I think he's still mooning after Tessa and he's wearing Bonnie like a hair shirt."

"A what?" Tanya asked. "What's a hair shirt?"

"It's a punishment." Ricky waved his hand at his sister. "They used to do it in the Middle Ages as a penance. This is not something you're going to be able to add to your fall line."

"Funny." Tanya slugged his shoulder. "And what about Tyler?"

"What about Tyler?" Ever since that night last winter when they slept together, he'd been cool and distant with her. She saw him in band meetings and there had been precious few of those. Over the summer, Sandy had had a party to vet Bear's new woman, but she'd skipped it because she hadn't had the courage to face Tyler in a social situation because she was afraid she'd screw up again.

"What's he been up to?"

"I'm told he's been hanging around with some of the local bands and partying a lot. He's Tyler. Mr. Nothing But a Good Time."

"Uh huh." Tanya stood up and stretched. "And on that note, I'm going to bed. Good night and Merry Christmas."

"Merry Christmas," Candy and Ricky said.

Candy stared into her drink. She'd managed about as much as Ricky had. Sandy had had a Christmas party, but she could swear Tyler had been avoiding her. He'd brought a bimbo with him. An honest to God cocktail waitress. The woman had been nice enough but knew she was out of her league. She'd been more fun to talk to than Bonnie who had spent the evening dropping hints about what she wanted for Christmas. Candy doubted she was happy with the wonderful family vacation in Thailand Brian had arranged.

"Are you comfortable here, Candy?" Ricky asked.

"Comfortable?"

"In Dad's house."

Candy laughed. "I've been here for almost a year now and every time I bring up looking for a place of my own, your dad comes up with a list of reasons why I shouldn't."

"Dad's spoiled. He always gets his way. That doesn't mean you're happy."

"I'm happy." This was happy, wasn't it? She had a challenging job working for herself doing something she loved. She lived in the lap of luxury for free. Tanya gave her beautiful clothes. She ate at the best restaurants. What was not to be happy about?

"You haven't dated anybody since you broke up with Frankie and it's not like nobody's asked."

Candy shrugged. "I haven't been interested in any of them."

Ricky crossed the room and sat down beside her. He brushed her hair off her face.

"Ricky." Men hated getting the like-a-brother-to-me line, and he was going to force it out of her.

"No, it's not that. I don't feel that way about you either."

"How do you know I don't feel that way about you?"

He cocked his head. "You eat breakfast every morning in an old T-shirt before you've brushed your hair or your teeth. Not attractive."

"You're a jerk."

"And you call me a jerk every chance you get." He mussed her hair. "But you know you're beautiful, right?"

"I don't know. I guess."

"You are, and if I didn't watch you eat breakfast every morning in a tattered Cleveland Indians T-shirt, I might even think you were hot myself." He kissed her forehead. "I pay attention to women. I've been watching them since I was a kid because Dad went through so many. Some women want to have fun. Some women want to settle down. Tessa and Tanya are party girls. You want to settle down. You have to find your guy and settle down with him."

"What if I found my guy and he didn't want to settle down with me?"

"He's an idiot. Find another one."

"Why the outpouring of advice from my not-brother?"

"It's Christmas. Consider it my gift to you."

"I thought your gift to me was the bracelet."

"That too. Merry Christmas." He stood up. "You going to bed?"

"In a little while. I'll see you in the morning in my tattered, unattractive T-shirt."

"It's a date."

After Ricky left the room, Candy stared at the tree. Of all the years she and Tyler dated, they'd only had one Christmas together. The first year, she'd been living with her dad and he'd still been at his parents. Every year she put up the tree, but that year Tyler had helped her. They'd baked cookies together and watched Christmas movies. It had been the best Christmas she could remember since her mom left. Maybe the best Christmas ever.

And here she was spending another Christmas wishing she could go back to that one.

She needed to make new Christmases. Finding another guy wasn't going to happen. Men left. They abdicated responsibility, died, or got distracted with some other part of their life that they thought was more important. No, if she wanted to settle down she needed to start her own family from scratch.

* * * *

June bounded up to her at Brian and Suzi's reception and started chattering in Chinese.

"Babe, you have to speak to me in English," Candy said. She glanced over her daughter's head. Joey had hung back letting his sister lead as usual.

June blinked. "Mama, can we play with Sonya and Andi?"

"Of course, but be careful with Sonya, she's little."

"I know."

"And stay where we can see you."

"Mama!" June scoffed as she flounced away.

"Why do your kids speak Chinese again?" Alex asked.

Candy smiled at Marc's wife wondering again how Marc ended up with the thin, serious English professor. He didn't deserve her. "I adopted them from China and I thought they should know about their own culture."

"And their nanny speaks Chinese."

"She barely speaks English and it's not the right dialect of Chinese, but it's at least Chinese. She's teaching June to write it, too. When Joey starts school, she'll start teaching him."

"And why did you adopt two kids from China?"

"Because I wanted a family and Mr. Right wasn't coming around."

Alex shook her head. "It still seems odd to me."

"You're not the only one. June's teacher didn't know what to make of it when she started hanging out with the ESL kids on the playground."

"She's very serious, isn't she?"

"June? Yes, she is. She was almost two when I adopted her and I think she has some memories of the orphanage. It wasn't a great place to be. Especially in comparison."

Alex looked around again and Candy knew what she was seeing. The white tent filled with round white linen covered tables, set with china and crystal the caterers were busy cleaning up. The whole spectacle, finished. Candy just saw another wedding, but one she hadn't put together.

"I wanted to thank you again for helping me with my wedding. I never could have done it without you." Alex fiddled with the white linen napkin on her lap. Smoothing it, folding it, and smoothing it again. Given enough time, the caterers wouldn't have to iron that one.

"No sweat. I'm starting to think I should go into wedding planning. I've done so many of these things lately."

"Are all the guys married now?"

"Everyone but Tyler." *Who had been loudly proclaiming all day that he was never getting married. Bless his heart.*

"Have you seen my sister?" Jason demanded.

"Jason, we were talking here."

"Excuse me." Jason bowed elaborately. "Pardon the interruption ladies, but have you seen Tessa?"

Candy gestured with her head toward the overlook. "She said she needed some air."

"Shit. She's taking this hard, isn't she?"

"Can you blame her?"

"Yes. She could have had Brian sixteen years ago if she'd wanted him."

"She didn't want Brian sixteen years ago." Candy swiveled her glass on the condensation ring it had left in the linen.

"No, she wanted Marc and every other rock star, movie star, and athlete she could get her hands on. No thanks to you." Jason scowled.

"I am not taking responsibility for the fact that your sister was youth-gone-wild like you boys were."

"You just happened to have all the connections."

Alex was watching all this like a tennis match.

"Why was it okay for you boys to tramp around as much as you wanted, but not for her? She was doing what you all were."

"That doesn't mean she gets to be pissy about it now."

Candy shrugged. "We all knew this wedding was going to be tough on a couple of people, just like yours was."

"Hey, Jody always knew I wasn't interested in her."

"And yet she dreamed."

Jason hunched his shoulders and then relaxed them with a gusty breath. "When are you coming out of semi-retirement? I don't like the new girl."

"Sarina is very good at what she does and when Joey starts school, I'll think about it."

Jason grumbled and stomped away.

"I missed something," Alex said.

"We've been stewing together for a long time. Jody had a crush on Jason before she ever met him and until he married Cassie and they started cranking out babies, she thought she still had a chance despite all signs."

"And Tessa?"

Candy scanned the tent. Unless Jody was outside, she'd ducked out early. Better than what she'd done at Jason and Cassie's wedding, which was to get drunk and cry. "Brian had a crush on Tessa and she wasn't interested in him so she let him down easy by starting a torrid affair with Marc."

"My Marc?"

"It was a long time ago. At the time the boys were partying pretty hardy. He's different now. They all are." Almost all of them. Not Tyler.

Alex nodded. "You guys know all about each other, don't you?"

"Just about. I met Tyler on the day of his audition." Candy couldn't stop the soft smile creeping across her lips remember that burnout wandering her section in the department store a million years ago.

"I feel like a carpetbagger." Alex wrapped her hands around the bowl of her wine glass.

Candy patted her arm. "We need fresh blood."

A wail headed her direction from the opening in the tent caught her attention. Tyler was headed her way with Joey in his arms and June trailing behind clutching his shirttail. She met them halfway.

"He fell and tore up his knees," Tyler said.

"Sit down and hold him so I can see." Joey's little moon face was screwed up with sobs. "Hush, sweetie. Mama's here."

The knees of his pants were shredded and bloody. Peeling them up, she could see the little pebbles imbedded in his skin. She brushed at them with a napkin, but Joey was clutching at her shoulders trying to climb into her arms.

"I'm sorry." Tyler hugged Joey, kissing his hair.

"What was he doing?"

"He climbed over the side of the slide and fell off."

Candy sighed. No doubt June or Andi did it first.

"Mama?" June whimpered.

"It's okay, sweetie. Joey hurt himself. It's not your fault."

"What happened?" Suzi crouched next to her, trying to push her white dress out of the way.

"Suzi, you don't want to get blood on your wedding dress." Candy gave in and let Joey climb into her lap.

"Oh don't worry about it." Suzi inspected Joey's knees. "Poor baby. The caterers have a first-aid kit. Tess! Tess, run and ask one of the caterers for the first-aid kit."

Brian's daughter took off at a run.

Of course the caterers had a first-aid kit. If Suzi didn't already have a very lucrative career of her own, Candy would have to hire her to work at her publicity firm.

"Maybe I should take him home." Joey's little body was hot and heavy and he was about to succeed in choking her.

"I hate for you to have to leave early." Suzi kept brushing gently at the dirt imbedded in Joey's knees.

"What's the matter?" Brian leaned over Suzi's shoulder. "Poor little guy."

"It's been a long day for them." Candy tried to struggle to her feet and ended up tipping over backward. Brian and Tyler both grabbed for her.

"I've got her," Tyler snarled.

"Fine." Brian took a step back with his hands up.

Tyler pulled Candy up with Joey still in her arms. "I'll drive you home."

"I can drive. June, go get Mama's purse."

"He's not going to let you go."

"He knows he has to sit in his car seat."

"Why are you arguing with me?"

Candy stared at him. Excellent question. If anyone else had asked if she wanted them to drive her home, she'd have agreed. But not Tyler. "I'm not. Joey will let go when we get to the car. He's already calming down."

"I think this is our cue to leave." Brian put his arm around Suzi's shoulders and pulled her away.

Tyler stepped closer. "Candy, let me take you and the kids home."

"I can do it myself. Joey isn't crying anymore."

"Candy."

Was he pleading? Why? "There's no point, Tyler. We'll be fine." She headed out of the tent to find June.

"Why not use the first-aid kit before you go? Get him taken care of. If he's stopped crying, maybe you can stay a little while longer." Tyler followed her.

In the corner of the tent nearest the opening, Candy spotted Jerry Eland with a girl on his lap. "Is that your date with Jerry?"

"What?" Tyler glanced in their direction. "Yeah, I kinda had that pegged."

"Okay." He hadn't changed. One woman was as good as another, and he'd have another within the hour.

June caught up to them and Tyler held out his hand. She took it without hesitation. Odd. June was usually very shy unless someone needed her help.

"Why don't I follow you home then? Make sure you get there okay."

"I know the way home. Find my keys and hit the button, June."

June fished through Candy's purse until she found the keys and deactivated the locks. Then she dropped the keys back in Candy's purse and reached for Tyler again. Really odd. June had time to open and close those locks a couple of times between here and the car. Normally she would hit that button a dozen times.

"Candy, why are you stonewalling me?"

"I'm not stonewalling you. My kids have had a long day and I'm taking them home. I don't need any help. I can manage two kids by myself for an evening. Wei might even be home already. You know the party is only half over."

"I don't care about the party."

"That's a first." Candy opened the driver's side rear door and settled Joey into his seat.

Tyler opened the other side and helped June strap herself in. "Is there some reason you don't want me to come to your house?"

"I didn't say that. I just said I didn't need to you to follow me home." Candy closed the door and so did Tyler.

"Okay."

Okay? He must be getting soft with age. "Well, it was nice seeing you again. Bye, Tyler."

He took a step back from the car and smiled.

"I like Tyler," June announced as Candy started the car.

"That's good."

"Do you like Tyler?"

"Tyler is a very old friend."

"But do you like him?"

"Yes, I like him." Too much. Still.

"He likes you."

"That's nice." He probably did in his way, but it wasn't enough. She needed a full-time partner, not somebody who thought it was his God-given duty to sample as many women as he could. True, he'd slowed down over the past few years, but she put that down to age.

"Can Andi and Sonya come play with us?"

"I will call their mom and see if we can arrange a play date." Might be nice to sit around with Cassie. She seemed nice enough. She'd certainly pulled Jason out of a hole. There'd been a sea of changes in the band over the last six or seven years. It was as if Bear found Maureen and all of them realized the joys of domestic bliss. All except Tyler.

Chapter 9

June chattered about the kids she'd met all the way home. Joey fell asleep. At the house he woke up crying. Wei was home, so she got June bathed and into her nightgown while Candy dealt with Joey's wound then got him bathed and into bed. June and Candy were playing Chutes and Ladders in the living room when the doorbell rang.

Candy checked the clock on the way to the door. Eight. Not terribly late, but she wasn't expecting anyone.

Tyler stood on the porch with a pizza box in his hands.

"What are you doing here?"

"I brought pizza." He stepped through the door past her.

"That doesn't answer my question."

"You left pretty early. I thought the kids might be hungry."

"Joey is in bed and June is about to go."

"Mama!" June wailed.

"No argument. Fifteen minutes then one story and lights out," Candy told her.

"But Tyler brought pizza."

"Yeah, Tyler brought pizza." Tyler put the pizza box on the table but didn't open it.

"One piece. A skinny one."

Wei came downstairs and asked June something in Chinese. June answered. Candy assumed it was about the pizza because Wei helped herself to a piece.

"Did I screw up?" Tyler asked. "I figured since you guys left so early the kids might be hungry."

"We didn't leave early."

"It seemed early."

"We run on a different clock than you do."

Tyler stroked June's hair and she grinned at him. "I guess so. You gonna have any?"

"It's a little late for me to eat, but you go ahead. Do you want a drink?" Why was he here? She hadn't even realized he knew where she lived.

"Sure."

Candy poured him a gin and tonic. She had to open new bottles of both and she wondered why she even kept it in the house. Nobody else drank gin and the tonic water would go flat before anyone finished it. Of course, she knew exactly what Tyler drank and how he liked it down to the brand of gin. She brought him the glass.

June was sitting in front of a half-eaten piece of pizza teaching Tyler Chinese under the humoring gaze of Wei.

"Not like that!" June squealed. "If you say it like that it means stupid. You have to say it like this. Mei *mei*."

"Mei *mei*."

Candy didn't hear the difference, but June and Wei both clapped so he must have gotten it right. "Finish up, June. You don't want to be grumpy tomorrow because you didn't get enough sleep."

"Yes, Mama." June focused on her pizza.

Candy glanced at Tyler, but he was watching June and she couldn't very well ask him what the hell he was doing here again because she wasn't going to get any straighter an answer out of him than she had at the door.

So what was he doing here? She hadn't seen much of him for a couple of years. Not since she told the band she was taking a sabbatical to raise the kids. Sarina ran the agency and there were two other publicists working there now so the profit from it was enough to keep her more than afloat. The last five years she'd spent creating her own home, not keeping tabs on their lives. She'd shown up for weddings, first Bear's, then Jason's. Then Marc met Alex and she'd help put that one together, but it didn't involve talking to Tyler at all except at the reception, which he'd appeared at each one with a different woman on his arm. According to all reports, he'd continued his rock star lifestyle without a hiccup. As all his friends settled down, he found new ones to party with.

Yet she'd kept a bottle of his favorite gin in the cupboard all these years even as she dated around looking for a reasonable facsimile and finding men who wanted a mother for their children or her connections or a warm bed or some combination thereof.

"Good night, Mama." June stood up, crumbling her paper towel in her hand. "Thank you for the pizza, Tyler." She said something to Wei in Chinese and Wei answered. Then June bounded toward the stairs.

"What did she say?" Candy asked Wei, stalling. Wei wouldn't hang around now that June was gone.

"She asks me for pizza breakfast. I say, we see." Wei stood and bowed. "Good night." She took the pizza box into the kitchen.

Candy stared at the empty space on the table. Now what was she supposed to say to him? He wasn't making any moves to go even though his fake errand had been completed.

"Nice wedding." Tyler wiped his fingers on a paper napkin and leaned back in his chair.

"Yeah. Very nice. She's very sweet. I remember helping her out when that sex tape thing happened a few years ago. She's nice. I think Brian will be a lot happier with her."

"The kids seem to like her a lot."

"They do."

Candy splayed her hands on the tabletop. Brian had screwed around on Bonnie all the time, but then Bonnie had done her fair share of screwing around, too. "He's gonna be faithful this time, right?"

"As far as I know." Tyler shrugged, twisting his glass on the table.

"I wouldn't want to see him messing with her head."

"He's not gonna mess with her head." Tyler scowled. "He's changed. People *can* change, you know."

"And yet more often than not, they don't." Candy stood up. She should check on the kids. June had had time to brush her teeth. She should be in bed by now.

"What's that supposed to mean?" Tyler stood too.

"Nothing."

He followed her to the stairs. "No, it doesn't. It doesn't mean nothing. Where are you going?"

"I have to check on the kids."

Wei was in June's room reading her a story and pointing out the characters as she did, though it looked as if June was already asleep. Joey had kicked off the covers and lay sprawled on his back, across the middle of the mattress. The huge bandages made his knees look worse than they were, but the wounds had only been superficial. She shifted him and spread the blanket over him again. It would be on the floor again by the time she went to bed.

Tyler stood in the hall, watching. "How did you end up with two Chinese kids?"

"I wanted kids and they needed a mom." Candy looked back at Joey. "I only planned on the one, but when I got there to pick him up I found June in the orphanage. The other kids all ran over and mobbed me, but she hung back. She was sitting at a little table playing with pebbles she'd picked up on the playground and kept in her pocket. They were the only toys she had. These pebbles. I couldn't leave her behind so I spent an extra two months in China getting the paperwork through and then I had to come home and buy a new house because I'd planned for one baby and one nanny, not a toddler, a baby, and a nanny."

"You and your strays." He draped his arm around her shoulders.

"Well, I do find them, don't I?" Candy let him lead her down the stairs. "What did you do to get my kids to like you so much?"

"They like me?"

"June does. She's usually very shy, but she isn't with you."

"I don't know. I played with them. They're nice kids."

"You never struck me as the kids type." She'd missed being with him. The weight of his arm anchoring her. Everybody thought he was flighty and goofy, but they didn't know him. He was a lot stronger than anyone knew. When there hadn't been anyone else, she'd been able to lean on him.

He stopped her in the middle of the living room and turned her toward him. "And you think you know me."

"I bet I know you better than most."

"I bet you do." He leaned down.

Candy shied away, taking a step backward. "Let's not go there again, okay?"

"Go where?"

"Look, I get it. We have history and we spent the day at a wedding. All your friends are married and you're feeling left out. That's not the best position to be making a decision from."

Tyler's jaw tensed. "What if I told you I made this decision a long time ago?"

"I'd say, where's the proof? Did it occur to you that one of my reasons for taking this sabbatical was so I wouldn't have to handle the press over your lifestyle?"

"My lifestyle?"

"A party every night." She reached behind her so she wouldn't stumble into the couch. "You really did change sexual partners more often than you changed your socks. Tell me, did you abandon your date at the reception with Jerry or did you at least make an attempt to make sure she could get home?"

"That's not fair."

"What? That you brought a social climber to a wedding and she climbed over you or that you should have to be responsible for her after she did it?"

"Jerry was taking her home."

"I'm sure."

"Candy, I'm not here to talk about my tragically poor taste in women."

Candy folded her arms. "Tragically poor taste."

"I didn't mean that the way it sounded."

"No doubt. Must have been a Freudian slip." Tears burned behind her eyes. His drink was still sitting on her table. "I don't know why you came here tonight, but I think it's time for you to go."

"Will you give me a minute?"

"No."

Tyler reached for her so she took another step back and bumped into the arm of the couch. She caught herself before she fell over. He grabbed for her, but she jerked away.

"Don't touch me."

"Candy, you're overreacting."

"Am I? I didn't think it was possible to overreact to the way you've tomcatted around for years."

"You can't hold that against me. We broke up. You didn't want me."

Candy slid around the arm of the couch so she could stand up. She needed to feel both her feet steady under her. "We weren't broken up when you started cheating on me."

"And it was what, twenty years ago?"

"Sixteen." Candy bit her lip wishing she could take that back. He didn't need to know she could remember to the exact date and time how long it had been.

"It was one time."

"As far as I'm concerned the number doesn't matter. And you were the one who wanted to get back together and have an open relationship."

"Never mind. This was stupid. I never should have come here." He marched to the door and started to slam it behind him, but caught it before it made a sound.

Candy sunk onto the couch. Sixteen years, three months, and ten days. Then a year later when she'd met them on the road and let him lure her back into his bed. And six years ago when she'd done it again. At least tonight she hadn't ended up sleeping with him. That was progress, wasn't it?

Because it felt more like a landslide.

* * * *

Tyler thought he was going to vomit. They were all sitting around comparing pictures of their kids and their wives and their honeymoons and their beautiful fucking lives, in Jason's beautifully decorated house. "Why are we even here?"

They all stared at him. Jason still had his mouth open.

"What's the matter with you?" Marc asked.

"We're not doing anything." Tyler stood up to pace. "We're not supposed to go into the studio for a fucking year. Suzi's got to have her goddamn baby first."

"Hey!" Brian yelped.

Tyler stopped in front of the window. The jibe was low. He shouldn't have said it, but for some reason he couldn't force himself to apologize.

"It's not our fault you got left behind," Jason said.

"Fuck off."

"We all grew up and you didn't."

Jason had been low too, but so very accurate. If fifteen years ago he'd told Candy he'd be completely faithful to her, her could have had her. No, wait, that was the second time, on the first tour. The first time was when he slipped with that girl while she was getting them their contract.

"Why don't you just talk to her?" Bear asked.

"Talk to who?" Jason asked.

"I tried. She's holding everything against me." Tyler leaned his forehead against the window.

"Everything from how far back?" Bear asked.

"Hello, who are we talking about?" Jason asked.

Tyler turned around. Jason was looking around the room as if he was lost. Brian and Marc didn't seem to have any more of a clue. "All the way."

"Wow. That's a lot of apologizing." Bear folded his hands. "You need kneepads. I bet Marc has some you can borrow."

"Pads? Sure, I have some catcher's pads." Marc started to stand and then dropped back into his seat frowning. "What do you need them for?"

"This would be a lot easier if he hadn't fucked her." Tyler jabbed his finger at Brian. Through Brian has sworn the next morning that nothing had happened and Candy—Candy wouldn't. He never needed to hear it from her because he knew better. So why was he picking this fight? "You know she always had a thing for you."

Brian reared back. "Who?"

"Candy."

"I never slept with Candy." Brian stood up. "Honest. I wouldn't do that to you. I know how it feels." He shot a look at Marc.

"Can we not bring up *all* the old garbage?" Marc said.

Tyler glared across the couches at Brian. For years he'd been imagining it. Even the bits that didn't make sense. Especially the bits that didn't make sense. It had been his explanation for why Brian and Jason were best friends, why Marc and Bear were best friends, and yet he was alone in the crowd. His personal mythology. "On the first tour, she came to my room and we got into a fight and she spent the rest of the night in your room."

"Jesus, the first tour? That night she threatened to quit? She spent the night in my room crying. All night long." Brian held out his hands. "I swear to you. I never had sex with Candy. Shit, that night I didn't even sleep. I was afraid if I took my eyes off her she'd either hang herself with the bed sheet or sneak back to your room and strangle you with it. And she never had a thing for me. I was friend-zoned by her before being friend-zoned was a thing."

"Wait a minute." Jason stood up. "You mean to tell me you're still hung up on Candy?"

Tyler clenched his teeth and stared at the carpet. It stemmed the tide of angry, irrational bullshit pouring out of his mouth too late.

"Am I the only one who didn't know?" Jason asked.

Marc and Brian grumbled that neither of them knew either.

"How could you miss it?" Bear asked. "He used to wear the same clothes for days on tour until Candy was coming. Then it was shower, shave, fresh clothes, the works. Every time somebody had a party, the first question out of his mouth was 'is Candy coming?' Every time we talk about something he wants to know what Candy would say."

"I thought it was because she was our publicist." Marc looked around the circle of faces. "I figured it was business."

"You would." Bear leaned back on the couch. "Man, you gotta talk to her."

"I've tried. She won't listen. I've been trying for the past couple of years. I even went to her house after your wedding reception last September." Tyler rubbed his fingers together. He'd always assumed fessing up to this would be the most horrible, painful experience possible, but so far it felt more like putting down a heavy load.

"Man, really? A couple of years?" Marc shook his head. "Alex is right. I don't pay attention."

Jason sucked his teeth. "You know what we could do."

"No." Brian scowled at Jason.

"We could—"

"No," Brian repeated. "Just forget it now."

"What do you mean, forget it? You don't even know what I'm going to say." Jason sat back down on the couch.

"And it doesn't matter. Every time you get a bright idea like that it blows up in somebody's face." Brian clapped his hands together. "Last time it was mine."

"But—"

"No."

"Fine." Jason flopped backward.

Tyler leaned on the windowsill. The quiet room wasn't at all uncomfortable. Ever since that morning after Brian slept with Candy—correction, Candy cried all night and Brian didn't sleep—he'd felt like he was cut off from them. For sixteen years, he'd been a member of this band and not really part of it. "I figured you were all pissed off at me that morning."

"What morning?" Jason asked.

"Keep up," Brian snapped. "The morning on the first tour when they got into that fight in the hall and she quit. Remember, Candy was half naked and crying in the hall of the hotel." He looked at Tyler. "Right?"

"Yeah. She was the one who got us really going. She packaged us and found the buyer and I kinda fucked up with her." Tyler glanced across the room at his beer. He didn't want it and didn't feel like crossing the room to get it, but he really wished he had something in his hands.

"I seem to remember telling you the next morning that nobody was mad at you." Brian leaned back against the couch.

"How could you not be? I was mad at myself."

"She was being unreasonable. She wanted you to give up all other women in the world for her." Bear frowned. "That made sense in my head."

"There were a lot of women at the time," Marc drained his beer. "Sixteen years ago. That first tour. Jesus. We were lining them up and picking out different favorites every night. Leaving the leftovers for those guys in Ground Force. Man, they hated us. We were jerks. But there were so many women."

"There still are." Brian laughed.

"I don't know what your excuses are, but my wife has a shotgun." Jason grinned as if he was proud of that fact.

"Groupies are like McDonald's," Tyler muttered. "There's always another one."

"That's my line!" Bear scowled.

"No, your line is 'why have hamburgers when you've got filet at home?'" Marc told him.

"Well, it's the same idea."

"Nobody was mad at you." Brian crossed the room and clapped Tyler on the shoulder. "You got stuck in a shitty position and she didn't quit in the end anyway. Seriously, when isn't somebody threatening to quit?"

"Okay." Marc rocked to his feet. "If we're all done with the caring and sharing, I need another beer. Anybody else?"

"Beer me," Bear said.

Jason raised his hand.

If nothing else, at least he had friends.

* * * *

Candy pushed the cart along the aisle. "Hurry up, June. You're falling behind."

"Sorry, Mama."

Candy glanced over her shoulder at her daughter. June was walking with her head down, shuffling her feet. It hadn't been a good day at school. She'd gotten in trouble for not paying attention and June hated to be in trouble. "Are you okay, sweetie?"

"I have a headache."

Joey grabbed a box of Cocoa Puffs off the shelf. "Mama, can I have this?"

"No, you have a full box at home." At least she thought there was a full box at home. Didn't matter. Joey would have forgotten all about it by the time they turned the corner. She should have stopped at the store before she picked up the kids at school, but she couldn't get away soon enough. Actors were such drama queens. Nothing was a little problem, it was all a major crisis that needed to be solved now! Well, she had her own crisis right now. The bake sale was tomorrow and she had nothing to contribute. "Where does it hurt, June?"

"What?"

"Your head." Boy, she really wasn't paying attention.

"All over. Can we go home?"

"Soon." Candy picked up two boxes of Rice Krispies, reconsidered, and added a third. Rice Crispy treats were always very popular. They'd go fast. Now to get the marshmallow. Where did they keep it in this store? Employees always seemed to disappear the moment she needed them. Her phone rang. If this was another fictional crisis—.

June's teacher's number was on the screen. Candy stopped the cart. She'd just talked to June's teacher half an hour ago about the bake sale, why would she call?

"Hello?"

"Hello Ms. Perry? This is Miss Marconi, June's teacher. I'm calling to let you know that Mark Kim was diagnosed with bacterial meningitis."

"Mark Kim?" Candy asked. She couldn't place the kid's face and couldn't figure out why she was trying.

"He's in our class and he went home sick at lunch. His mother called to tell us it's meningitis. You may want to get June checked."

Candy stared at June who was still looking at the floor. "What are the symptoms?"

"Headache, stiff neck, spiking fever, sensitivity to light, vomiting."

Headache. June had just complained about a headache. On the way here she'd said it was too bright out even though she was wearing her sunglasses. A song off Touchstone's first album came on the grocery store's overhead play. Candy touched June's forehead. Hot. Too hot.

Candy dropped her phone into her purse and hoisted Joey out of the cart. "Come on, we have to go." She grabbed June's hand.

"What about the shopping?" June trotted behind her.

"It can wait." Candy pushed through the grocery store doors. Where was the car? Where was the nearest hospital?

"But I need it for school tomorrow."

"You aren't going to school tomorrow."

"I don't feel good, Mama." June pulled her hand away and stopped.

"We're going to the doctor right now."

June leaned over and threw up careful not to get any on her clothes.

Candy set Joey down. Miss Marconi said vomiting. This couldn't be happening. She'd been fine this morning. Miss Marconi had said she was a little out of it today in school. The kid in her class who brought the disease in had gone home at lunch. How could this happen so fast? "It's going to be okay, sweetie." She wiped June' mouth with a tissue.

"Mama!" Joey clutched her arm.

"Joey, move back." God, what if he was infected? What if both of them had it? People died of meningitis.

"Is everything okay?" Someone asked behind her.

Candy looked around. She didn't recognize the face and thought she should. Hell, it was Malibu. Who lived here that wasn't famous? The sun behind him wasn't helping. "My daughter is sick and I need to take her to the doctor. Can you help me get my kids into the car?"

"No problem. Where are you parked?" He started to scoop June up.

"No!" Candy sucked in a breath. Would he help her if he knew? What if he had kids of his own at home? He could take it home to them. She couldn't get two kids, one sick, in the car by herself though. Wei was visiting family in China now. "It might be meningitis."

"All right. Why don't you carry her and I'll bring your boy? Come on, sport." The man held out his hand.

Joey studied him, clinging to Candy's pant leg as she picked up June.

"It's okay, babe. I'm right here," Candy told her son.

At the car she had to put June down to find her car keys. Her rescuer buckled Joey into his seat as she strapped in June. June looked miserable and her little body radiated fever. "Mama, I don't feel good."

Candy pulled a plastic bag out of the seat pocket and handed it to June. "We're going right to the doctor. You'll be all better soon."

"Are you Luke Skywalker?" Joey asked the savior.

He laughed and closed the door. Over the roof, he looked at Candy. "Are you sure you're going to be all right to drive?"

"I'll be fine. Thank you." Candy dove into the driver's seat.

She made it to the hospital in record time. Carrying June, and trailed by Joey, she went straight to the admitting desk. June was mumbling in Chinese and Joey was crying. "My daughter has a fever and a headache and she's throwing up. One of the kids in her class has been diagnosed with meningitis."

The nurse nodded. "Right through here. We're going to need your permission to do some tests."

"Anything. Whatever you need." Candy lay June on the white papered table the nurse indicated. She looked so small and helpless. Joey wrapped his arms around her hips. Another nurse bustled in and shooed her away from the table so she could examine June. A third person came in with a sheaf of forms for her to fill out.

"Is there someone you can call?" The second nurse asked. "The child's other parent?"

Candy stared at the women. Other parent? June didn't have another parent. All she had was Candy and Wei who was in China. Maybe she should have let the guy from the grocery store drive her to the hospital. She found her phone and scrolled through the numbers. So many people. Clients, acquaintances, friends. Who do you call when your child is in the hospital with a life-threatening illness? Her finger paused over one number. He would come. She knew he would come.

* * * *

Tyler heard his phone ringing and couldn't remember where he put it. He wandered through the house for three rings before he located it on the dresser in the bedroom. Why was Candy calling? Jason hadn't done anything unauthorized had he? "Hello?"

"Tyler, June is sick."

Her voice was all wrong. Hollow. She sounded like the night her dad hit her and he had to take her out of there. This was probably how she sounded when she called Ronnie the night Frankie hit her. "What do you mean, June is sick?"

"She—a boy in her class has meningitis. She said she had a headache, but I thought she was upset because she got in trouble at school today and then she threw up in the parking lot." Candy sobbed.

Tension wrapped around Tyler's vocal chords. Meningitis was bad. "Candy, where are you?"

"St Lucy's."

That was bad. Hospital bad. Chills ran down his arms. Christ, he hated hospitals. Tyler slid his feet into sandals as he grabbed his wallet and car keys. "Are you in the kids' ward or emergency or what?"

"Emergency."

"I'll be there in fifteen minutes. Is Joey with you?"

"He's here. Wei is in China."

Great. No nanny support. "Tell me what's going on." He paused at the door long enough to set the alarm and lock up then switched her to speaker on the way to the car so he could text Tessa. From the sound of Candy, she was not going to be able to fill out her own paperwork.

Candy recited a blow-by-blow of exactly what was happening in the exam room that looped back on itself. As long as she kept talking, Tyler didn't care what she said. In the background he could hear Joey crying.

Traffic conspired against him. The fifteen minutes he'd promised stretched into twenty-five before he waded through the mob scene to the admitting desk. Half the city seemed to be in the emergency room where seven people in scrubs were trying to feel everyone's glands and take everyone's temperature at the same time. The guard at the door had shoved a surgical mask into his hand when he walked through the door and a kid sneezed on him. Candy wasn't even talking to him now. A nurse seemed to be trying to make her understand that she needed to hold June while they did a spinal tap and Candy wasn't understanding.

"My friend brought her daughter in here. Candy Perry. The girl's name is June Perry. She's Chinese."

"You could hang up the phone." The admitting nurse pointed a long red nail at the cell phone wedged against his ear.

"No, I really can't. I've been talking to Candy since she called to tell me where she is and I'm sort of afraid of what will happen if I hang up."

"Are you the child's father?"

"The child is an orphan. Candy adopted her."

The admitting nurse sighed. "Did you adopt her?"

"No."

"I can't let you back there unless you're the child's legal guardian or her pediatrician and I'm pretty sure you're not her pediatrician."

Tyler scowled at the woman. Based on what he was hearing through the phone, the conversation had started below the Mason-Dixon and was now headed farther south. The nurse might have better luck if she spoke Chinese because then Joey might understand at least. Tyler walked past the desk and pushed through the doors.

"Hey! You can't go back there! Security!"

The whole area was a warren of over-bright little rooms, half of which were blocked by curtains down the middle. He held the phone a little away from his ear trying to pick Candy's voice out in the hall.

A huge black guy grabbed his arm. "Buddy, you can't be back here."

"Listen man, my ex-girlfriend is back here with her little girl who's really sick and she's fallin' apart. She called me. You know how it is."

The guard drew a deep, authoritative breath. "Yeah, come on. She the one with the two Chinese kids?"

"Yes."

The guard led him down another hall to yet another over-bright room. He pulled the curtain back to reveal Candy open-mouthed and baffled by what the nurse was trying to tell her, the nurse rapidly reaching the end of her tether, Joey wrapped around Candy's hips sobbing like a baby and June laying hopefully half-asleep on a table.

Candy still had the phone pressed to her ear, but when the curtain moved, she dropped it and threw herself into his arms. "They want to put a needle in my baby's back!"

"Tyler!" Joey switched to Tyler's legs.

The nurse picked up the phone and rolled her eyes at the guard.

"Honey, they wouldn't want to do it if they didn't need to." He'd only been half paying attention to the explanation, but the nurse had repeated it so often he knew what was going on. "They've got to make sure it's meningitis. The nurse is going to roll her on her side and you need to hold her still so she can get some fluid from June's spine." Just saying the words made his skin crawl.

"I can't. I can't."

Tyler didn't think he'd ever heard those words from her. Candy could do anything. But her eyes were wild and her hands were shaking. She looked like a cheap imitation of herself.

"You want me to do it? You take care of Joey. I'll take care of June."

Candy nodded. "I can't watch."

Tyler's stomach twisted. Watch? There didn't seem to be any option. "Take Joey out to the hall and we'll let you know when it's over." He peeled Joey away and handed him off to Candy, who took him into the hall.

"Thank you," the nurse groaned. "Some moms can't handle it when their kid is really sick. I'm gonna roll her onto her side and you keep her still. You can sit on that stool."

Tyler hooked the stool closer to the table with his foot. "Hi, mei mei. Don't feel good, huh?"

June tried to shake her head but winced. "My neck hurts."

"I know. The nurse is going to do something to help fix that. Okay?" He brushed her hair off her face. Then he braced himself. At least June wouldn't be able to see the needle they were using. It looked about a foot long and as big around as a cannon.

The nurse hesitated, frowning. "Are you the child's father?"

Tyler glanced toward the hall. Candy was out there in pieces with Joey. He was tempted to point out that June was Chinese and he was standard North American mutt, but for some reason the easy joke wouldn't come. "It's complicated."

The nurse grunted. "Isn't it always."

* * * *

Six hours later they'd admitted June to the PICU. Brian and Suzi had taken Joey to their house. Tyler combed his fingers through Candy's hair. "Babe, why don't you come eat something? There's nothing we can do here."

"She looks cold," Candy murmured.

Tyler peered through the window. June was flush with fever, and according to the nurse, they'd put a cold blanket on her to keep her body temperature down. The last thing she was was cold. "There's a whole team of people here dedicated to making sure she's as comfortable as possible."

"I don't want her to be comfortable. I want her to be okay."

A few other parents lingered in the hall outside the windows of their own sick children's rooms murmuring to one another. Nurses buzzed around the desk behind them. Tyler wished he had a guitar so he'd have something to do with his hands. Standing here, staring through this window was maddening.

There was nothing he could do beyond what he'd already done. He'd called everyone. For the first couple of hours there had been a steady stream of people coming to find out what happened and lend support, but they'd dried up after a while. Ronnie and Ricky were on tour doing a show in Florida tonight. Tanya was in Paris, but she'd had someone from her boutique deliver some sunglasses to give the staff. Maureen had taken them home to make gift bags with certificates to Cassie's campground, free dinner coupons at the Potterville diner, and the variety of things Candy's clients had flooded her office with when word circulated. Hollywood didn't send flowers. They made swag bags for the staff.

Sarina had displayed a sudden germ phobia and wouldn't come to the hospital, but she'd been calling for hourly reports and to give her own. She seemed to be trying to do an entire year's work in one evening. Not that Candy knew anything about it. Tyler had been fielding her calls because when she did talk to people none of what she said made sense.

They couldn't do anything either. June was under professional care and Candy was rooted to the floor outside her room.

The little Indian doctor in charge of June turned away from the desk and walked toward them. "Ms. Perry?"

Candy blinked at her twice and then turned back to the window.

The doctor started talking as though Candy was paying attention. From what Tyler had seen, she had a lot of practice doing that. "Your daughter still has a very high fever. We are keeping her cool, but we are going to keep her in the PICU overnight for observation. These first few hours are critical. Tomorrow we will hopefully be able to move her to a regular isolation room. You should go home, get some rest and see to your other child."

"She doesn't have her rabbit." Candy sniffled.

"She will sleep fine tonight without it. You need to keep up your strength and take care of your son."

"My son?" Candy blinked at Tyler. "Where is Joey?"

"Brian and Suzi took him home."

"Is he sick?"

Tyler glanced at the doctor who shrugged as if she totally understood Candy was on another planet. "They tested him, remember? He's fine. He's staying the night with Brian and Suzi."

"Oh good. He'll like that." And her gaze went right back to June through the window.

"She should eat something." The doctor bobbled her head side to side. "This will run its course in seven to ten days, but we have to watch for complications. She's going to need all her strength."

Tyler nodded. "I'll do what I can."

"If you would like, I can prescribe her a sedative to put her to sleep."

"I'd have to get her to swallow something to get that in her." He brushed his fingers through Candy's hair again. "She'll snap out of this. It's the shock. Give her some time."

The doctor nodded. "All right. Please let the nurses know if you need anything."

Candy slumped against him. "I should have made sure she had all the shots they said she had."

Too bad that didn't win the non sequitur of the week award.

"They had to have so many shots. I didn't want to make them suffer more needles to get blood tests for the shots they told me they had. If I had, maybe she wouldn't be so sick. There's got to be an immunization for this." Candy flattened her hand on the window. "This is my fault."

"Candy, half the kids in June's class are sick. I think if there was an immunization they'd be fine."

"Mark had measles."

Measles?

"His mother didn't get him the immunizations because she believed they caused autism so he got measles and then he got this."

And another sharp left. "Candy, I don't think you can blame Mark's mother. Let's go down to the coffee shop and get a bite to eat. June will still be here when we get back and they said you can borrow a pager so they can page you if something happens."

"Something might happen."

"Which is why they give you the pager." Tyler gave her an experimental tug. She moved with him so he guided her to the nurses' desk for a pager and then down to the coffee shop in the first floor atrium. Leaving her at a table with the pager, he went to the counter and ordered her a half-caf skinny mocha heavy on the whipped cream, a bottle of water, a roast beef sandwich, and a bowl of New England clam chowder. One of the four should entice her.

"This is my fault," she said when he carried the tray back to the table.

"No it isn't." Tyler arrayed the food in front of her to see if she was still with him enough to be tempted. She didn't even seem to notice it.

"I should have had her get another set of shots even though it meant more needles. A couple of needles then would have saved her all this."

"You can't know that and I don't think the doctors would have let you anyway." He nudged the soup closer. He'd never seen her refuse clam chowder. Of course she never let a good mountain of whipped cream pass by either and hers was melting.

"They would do what I told them to do."

"I don't think even you can summon that kind of power." Tyler placed the spoon in her hand. "Eat your soup."

"I'm not hungry."

"Yes, you are. Eat." He took the pager out of her other hand.

"I think Mark Hamill helped me get the kids in the car."

And another winning non sequitur for the books. "Really? Could have been. He lives around here, doesn't he?"

"Joey asked him if he was Luke Skywalker." Candy looked around. "Where's Joey?"

"We sent him home with Brian and Suzi, remember?"

"Oh yeah." She took a sip of the soup. "What are you doing here?"

"You called me."

"But you are terrified of hospitals."

"And you still called me."

She nodded and took another swallow. "I should go back upstairs. June might wake up."

Tyler grabbed her wrist. "Finish the soup first."

"Bully."

He turned her hand over and rubbed his thumb across her palm. "Only in your best interest. Finish the soup. We can take the coffee and sandwich to go."

"Aren't you going to eat?"

"I'm not hungry."

"Right." She shoved the sandwich toward him with a ghost of a smile.

"Bully." He unwrapped it.

"Only in your best interest."

She ladled the rest of the soup into her mouth in silence, one eye on the pager. "Thank you for coming."

"Not a problem." He licked horseradish off his fingers. He still wasn't sure why she'd called him. Why, in a blind panic, would his number be the one she picked? She didn't seem to know either so he wasn't going to push it. "Are you going to go home tonight? Try to get some sleep?"

"I want to be here in case she wakes up. Should I call Joey?"

"It's nine-thirty. You'll wake him up."

"I miss him." She pushed away the bowl and put her head down on her arms. "I'm a terrible mother."

"You're a great mother." He put his arm across her back. "Candy, kids get sick. It's no one's fault. You are not responsible for everything that happens."

"I couldn't hold her when they did the spinal tap. You had to do it."

Tyler winced. Holding June as she cried and pleaded with him to make them stop had not been a lifetime highlight, but he'd do it again. June had needed somebody and so had Candy. "You needed to take care of Joey. June understands. I think the only thing you really did that might damage them was give them names what had the same first letter. That's just too cute."

Candy made a noise that could have been a laugh or a sob. "Not funny."

Must have been a laugh.

"I'd already decided I was going to name the baby after Joe when I found June. Lo June Ghou."

"I guess it's a good thing she already had a name or you'd have probably tagged her with Goldie."

"Shut up." She swatted him and reached for the coffee. "I'm going back upstairs."

"She isn't going to wake up." Tyler put her bowl back in the tray and picked up the end of the sandwich. "The doctor has her on something to make her sleep."

"I need to be there for her."

Tyler followed her to the elevator. *And I need to be here for you.*

Chapter 10

Candy came to slowly. She was hot, but cradled tightly on a narrow bed. Or maybe a couch. She sat up and nearly fell off the edge. Tyler was asleep, holding her on an ugly gray couch. He shifted when she moved, but didn't wake up. The last thing she remembered was standing in the hall watching June sleep through the window. Another couple curled together on the opposite couch. Leaving him sleep, she went back to June. She was asleep, too. Her face didn't look as flushed now.

A nurse put her hand on Candy's shoulder. "You and your husband should go home and get some real rest. Your daughter will be fine. She's responding really well. In the morning we'll move her to a regular room."

"I'd rather stay."

"Most parents do, but it really doesn't do any good." The nurse squeezed her shoulder. "At the very least, go back to sleep. You both look exhausted and you're going to want to be on your toes when we move her to her room. I'll wake you if anything changes."

Candy checked June, who was deeply asleep. She smiled at the nurse and headed back to the lounge. Tyler was still sleeping on his back with his arm hanging off the side of the couch. The nurse had called him her husband and she hadn't bothered to correct her. She crawled back into Tyler's embrace, wrapping his arms around her. He shifted and kissed her forehead. It was safe here, and quiet.

When doctors performed the spinal tap, she'd stood in the hall listening to June cry while Tyler crooned to her. Where or why he'd learned the lyrics to "Do You Want to Build a Snowman" from the *Frozen* cartoon, she didn't know. She couldn't have gone into that room for a million dollars. All she wanted to do was smack the nurse's hands away. But Tyler had been so strong. Thank God she'd had him to call. This was a much higher order of favor than asking somebody to help you move. *Hey, can you come to the hospital and hold my kid while they do a spinal tap on her and then stay all night making sure I stay sane?* What could she ever do to pay him back? Cookies were not going to cut it.

Candy closed her eyes. Something would come to her. She needed a little rest so she could think straight and then she'd start working on a way to pay him back.

* * * *

"But I have to go back to school tomorrow," June whined. "I'm missing everything. I'm going to fall behind."

"You're in second grade. You have time to catch up." Candy walked out with the tray. A week and a half after she went into the hospital, June was still too tired to sit up for very long and she wanted to go to school. Candy didn't remember being that serious in elementary school. High school yes, but not second grade. Joey followed her down the hall. "And what do you want?"

"I'm bored. I want to play with June."

"June is too tired to play with you. She needs to stay in bed. Besides, Brett and Tessa are coming to take you to Disneyland in a little bit." And none too soon. Candy had taken time off from work to take care of June. When she'd first brought the kids home she'd taken off four years, just returning a few months ago. How had she done it? Eight days and she was climbing the walls. At least Wei would be home in a few days. None too soon.

The doorbell rang.

Joey ran for it screaming.

"Joey, don't you open that door. You know you're not allowed." Candy followed him. He hadn't opened the door, but he'd climbed on the chair beside it and pulled back the curtain. Brett was on the other side of the window mashing his open mouth on the glass. Candy opened the door. "You know that glass is filthy."

"Considering what's been in his mouth, I wouldn't worry about it." Tessa smirked at Brett who stuck out his tongue.

"Tessa, little pitchers." Candy put her hand on Joey's head.

"It's only dirty if you have a dirty mind." Tessa threw Brett a dark look. "Last weekend he picked up a hotdog that fell in the grass and ate it."

"I picked the grass off." Brett grabbed Joey. "Are you ready for Disneyland, buddy?"

"Yeah!"

"Go put your shoes on." Candy pointed toward the stairs.

Tessa stepped inside. "Tyler here?"

"Why would Tyler be here?"

Tessa cocked one eyebrow at her.

"He called to say he was coming over in a little while to see June."

"To see June."

"Yes, to see June." Candy folded her arms. Couldn't be for any other reason.

"Right."

"Tyler and I have been friends for a long time."

"I'm your friend and I didn't sit at the hospital with you for three days."

Candy tugged at the hem of her T-shirt. It was one of Touchstone's old concert T-shirts and it had stains on the front from when she was trying to switch Joey from formula to baby food. "He was there for June."

"He was there for you. June had a team of professionals watching her around the clock. You wouldn't eat, wouldn't sleep, and frankly, didn't make any sense for the first twelve hours. I've had better conversations with dogs."

"My daughter was in the intensive care unit."

"I know and who was the first person you called?"

Candy had never figured out why she called Tyler. It had seemed like the only option at the time, but in retrospect, it was a little odd. She should have called Ronnie and if she'd remembered Ronnie was on tour, she should have tried Sandy next. So why had she called Tyler?

Brett zoomed through with Joey in his arms.

"I'm Superman, Mama!" Joey squealed on the way past.

"Remember last year when I was agonizing over Brett and we had that conversation about boundaries and limitations?" Tessa asked. "Your boundaries are too tight and you don't know your limitations."

"What's that supposed to mean?"

"It means you have such stringent boundaries you won't let anyone in. You have managed to keep everyone at arm's length the entire time I've known you. You judge every relationship on who's using who and is it equitable. And you don't accept that you have limitations."

"That's not true. I hired a nanny because I knew I had limitations. I knew I couldn't raise two kids on my own." Through the door she could see Brett putting the car seat in the backseat of Tessa's car. Before they left, she'd have to check it and make sure he'd done it right.

"Let's break this down." Tessa held up her hand so she could tick her points off on her finger. Sometimes having a lawyer for a friend sucked. "You adopted two Chinese kids. You had a more than full time job running your office and you wanted the kids to speak their native language. Therefore, you *hired* someone to teach the kids Chinese and as a byproduct, help you take care of them. I helped you with the contract. You made sure it was a very fair agreement. Wei probably has the best employment conditions of any unskilled worker alive and all because you didn't want to feel you would owe her anything at the end."

"What does that have to do with Tyler?"

"Tyler is the only person I've ever seen you let in and it drives you crazy."

"Tyler and I are friends."

"Yeah." Tessa put her hands on her hips. "You know, I've been watching this show for twenty years now and it's been in reruns for the last fifteen. It's getting boring."

"It hasn't been that long, and I can't trust Tyler. Not in a serious relationship. He's cheated on me before and he'll do it again." A cold spot formed behind Candy's breastbone. She could still remember sitting in Callisto's living room with a piece of pizza in her hand listening to Tessa and Jason scream at one another while Tyler stared at her like his life hung in the balance of whether she took a bite or not. She hadn't, she recalled. She'd put the pizza down and locked herself in her room.

"You know that was twenty years ago, right?"

"Seventeen."

"And what does it tell you that you remember that detail? I bet you know exactly what date and time, too."

It had been after work. He'd picked her up outside the office and taken her to show her that shitty apartment he'd rented before they got pizza and went back to Callisto's. On a Wednesday. The weather had been cool and overcast, but not so cold she needed a jacket.

Tessa hugged her. "I love you, babe, but you are the biggest bundle of neurosis I've ever met and my brother is Jason Callisto."

"And look who you're living with." Candy gestured toward the car. Brett had finished putting the car seat in and gotten Joey buckled in. Maybe she didn't need to check it. Brett was good about that stuff. As looney and irresponsible as he could be, he minded the important stuff.

"You're making my point for me. See you later. We'll bring the boy home wiped out." Tessa headed for the driveway.

"Don't let him have too much sugar or he'll get sick."

"Brett can clean it up. He'd be the one giving the kid sugar anyway." Tessa waved over the roof of the car and climbed in the driver's seat.

Funny, Tessa still drove.

Tyler had to wait on the street as they pulled out. As always, his timing was impeccable. He parked in front of the garage. "Hey, you unload Joey?"

"Tessa and Brett volunteered to take him to Disneyland."

"Because everybody wants to go to Disneyland on Tuesday afternoon." Tyler strolled around the front of his car. He had a gift bag in his hand from Toys "R" Us.

"He's four. He's up for Disneyland anytime." Candy couldn't remember the last time she'd really looked at Tyler. The image she'd always held in her mind was of him as a gangly boy singing for the biggest local band. Sometime between then and now his shoulders had gotten broader and his face had firmed. He had an air of confidence about him that he'd been very lacking when she met him.

He stopped at the door. "What?"

"Nothing."

"You're staring at me."

"Was I?" Candy smiled. Had he gotten taller too? He seemed taller.

Tyler angled past her. "I brought a little something to keep June distracted."

"What is it?"

"Wii."

Candy followed him down the hall. "Tyler, that game system requires a lot of movement. She needs to stay in bed." And Tessa thought he'd changed. He was the same irresponsible, thoughtless—

"The kid at the store loaded me up with point and shoot games."

"Oh. You know, you all spoil her. That flat screen Ronnie had installed in her bedroom is nicer than the one we have in the family room."

"So switch it out when she gets better." Tyler turned into June's room. "Hey beautiful!"

"Tyler!"

Why was June so happy to see him? She knew why Joey got so excited to see him. Joey loved anybody who would throw him in the air, but June was more selective, and she was always happy to see Tyler. Candy stopped outside the door and listened as June unwrapped her newest treasure. The kid now had enough entertainment to be bedridden for a year. She chattered delightedly as Tyler hooked it up for her. Candy could hear Tyler explaining which games she could play now, which she should save for later, and that the game would have to go into the family room when she got better. He sounded so much like a dad. So responsible.

Candy went back down to the kitchen. With both kids occupied, she had a little time to get some work done.

But not enough.

"What are you doing?" Tyler sat down at the table.

"Sorting out some work so I'll be ready to get back to it first thing next week." Candy closed her planner. "June ignoring you in favor of the game?"

"No. We played a couple of rounds and she got tired so we put in a movie. She was asleep before Simba started singing about how great it is to be king."

Candy studied his face. He had come right to the hospital when she called him. He had stayed for three days. Someone had brought them changes of clothes. He'd been here almost every day since she brought June home. "Why did you come when I called you?"

"You didn't call me. I called you this morning and said I would be by." Tyler picked up a headshot. "New client?"

"I mean at the hospital. Why did you come?"

Tyler put down the picture. "I don't know. You've been telling me what to do for most of my life. I guess I'm used to obeying."

"That's not funny."

"Well, why don't you tell me what you want?"

Candy stared at him wanting to rail, but not having the words. She clenched her jaw.

"Are you okay?" He put his hand on her wrist. "It's been a pretty stressful couple of weeks here. Maybe you should take a nap, too. I can hold down the fort."

"Why?" The wail in her voice surprised both of them. Her eyes burned.

"Candy." Tyler stood and pulled her into his arms. "You are really stressed out. Come sit down and let me make you a cup of tea."

"No. No!" Candy pulled away from him. "Stop taking care of me."

"Okay. Then what do you want me to do?"

"I want you to tell me why you keep coming back. Why are you here now? Why did you come to the hospital and stay for three days? Why did you meet me at the airport when I came back from China with the kids? Why did you check on me when I moved into Ronnie's after I broke up with Frankie?"

Tyler rubbed his face. "You really need a cup of tea."

"I need answers."

"You *need* to lower your voice or you're going to wake up June."

Candy bit her lip. "I want to know why you keep coming back."

"Because I love you."

"You can't."

"Sh!" Tyler scowled. "Why can't I?"

"Because you slept with every available female rather than be with me."

"First of all, I slept with them. I didn't love them. Second of all—" Tyler pointed at her. "Okay, there isn't a second. But I never loved any of them. I was a stupid little boy. You are the only woman I ever loved."

"How could you sleep with them if you didn't love them?"

"It's really easy and there was only that one before we broke up. You never gave me a second chance."

"How was I supposed to give you a second chance when I had to wade through women to get to you at all?"

"I know what number two is now. Second of all, it was a long time ago."

"It was last year."

"No, last year you were still punishing me for Jennifer what's-her-name seventeen years ago. Which most people think is a long time."

"Now you're going to wake June."

Tyler walked away.

"Where are you going?"

"The kitchen."

Candy followed and watched him put a mug of water in the microwave. He had a second one on the counter. "What are you doing?"

"It's not obvious?"

"Then why are you doing it?"

"I don't know. Tell me, is it a conspiracy? Am I crazy? Maybe there's something else going on I haven't considered that explains all my actions for reasons other than why I think I did them." He lowered his voice. "Should we call Fox Mulder?"

"Tyler." Candy covered her face with her hands.

"Candy, why can't you believe that I love you? Every single love song I've ever written has been about you." He leaned on the counter. "I get why you were afraid. What I don't get is why you're still afraid. I'm here. I'm always here. I'm like fucking Old Faithful."

"You were Party Central for nearly two decades."

"Not even." The microwave chimed. "I admit, I had my fun, but that's all it was and we were not together. You can't hold it against me like I was cheating on you when we were not a couple. If you'd give me a break and let me back in I could prove it to you. I'm ready now. I've been ready for a couple of years just waiting for an opening." He put the other cup in the microwave and dropped a tea bag in the first one.

Candy wrapped her arms around herself. "You're going to leave me."

"What makes you think that when you admit I'm always here?" He pulled her arms apart and wrapped them around his waist. "Candy, how many women have I dropped everything and run to the hospital for? The hospital. You know how I feel about germs and needles."

"We almost had to sedate you to get your shots the first time you went overseas." Candy pressed her cheek against his chest. He really was much more solid than she remembered. "I thought you were going to break my hand you were squeezing it so hard."

"You're lucky I didn't pass out when they did the spinal tap on June. Did you see that needle?"

"It *was* huge."

He stroked her hair. "Can I ask a dumb question?"

"What?"

"Where are we now?"

Candy twisted her head so she could see his face without stepping away. He wore no expression, waiting. "I love you."

"And you're going to give me another chance?"

"Let's just take it easy. Everybody is going to have to get used to us again."

"I'm a very patient man."

Candy laughed. "I've noticed."

"Hey Candy? How much money do you have?"

"On me or in the bank?"

"Both, because I'm about to lose a lot of bets."

Epilogue

"Well, I'm glad to see the two of you finally got back together." Sandy raised his glass to the happy couple. "After nearly twenty years of watching this little soap opera, I was going to be really angry if I died before the two of you figured this out."

"Sandy, you're going to outlive us all," Jason said.

Sandy grunted.

Candy brushed her hands over her simple cotton dress.

"I can't believe you wouldn't let me design you something better," Tanya grumbled. "Honestly, who gets married in a cotton sundress in somebody's backyard?"

"The person who's arranged dozens of weddings."

"Dozens. It hasn't been dozens."

Candy started ticking off on her fingers. "Brian's first one. Jason and Cassie's. Connie's. I did all of Marc's first one, and helped out a lot with Alex. Mrs. Callisto's and that postmaster in Potterville. Bear and Maureen's. All four members of Send Down. Tessa and Brett."

"Still not dozens."

"You act like you're the only people on Earth. I have other friends and other clients who think I'm a full service PR and wedding service. Gayle Rubio has been married four times already and I suspect she's working on number five now. Jerry Eland and that twit with that stupid song about short skirts."

"I wrote that song," Marc grumbled.

"Doesn't make it good." Jason leaned back in his chair.

"It was a huge hit."

"Played at every fair in the country, but it sucked."

Marc leaned forward. "It doesn't have to be high art. It was a good solid song."

"It was a ditty with a catchy chorus."

Tyler combed his fingers through her hair. "They're going to be at this for a while."

"As long as they aren't telling stupid drummer jokes, I don't care." Maureen stood up. "Anyone need a refill?"

"Maureen, be a dear and get me another cup of coffee. I have an announcement to make." Sandy sat up straighter.

"I do not like the sound of this." Ronnie held up his glass.

"Here, I'll help you, Maureen. I need another Coke anyway." Alex took Ronnie's glass.

"Coke. I am dying for a Coke," Suzi moaned.

"After the baby is born." Brian hugged her.

"Can she have Coke while she's nursing or will it still hurt the baby?" Cassie asked.

Brian held up a hand. "Don't go there."

"Come on, Cassie. A nice even three. Brian's getting ahead of me." Jason nuzzled Cassie's neck. "Think how much fun it'll be trying."

"Like we don't try plenty now." Cassie pushed him away with her shoulder and then leaned back in his embrace.

Candy surveyed the group. The guys in the band and Sandy she had known most of her life. Ronnie, Ricky and Tanya, not much less. The band's wives had come along later, but they fit into the group as if they'd been there from the beginning. Their collective kids squealed and laughed at the far end of the yard. Andi, Sonya, June, Joey, and Bri had squirt guns. Tess had Tessa and Brett's newly adopted Bulgarian infant in her arms, cooing as though the world revolved around him. If she squinted the right way, she could see Joe standing in the back of the group, a pleased smile on his face as all his plans came together. Too bad he couldn't really be here to see it.

"Here you go, Sandy." Maureen handed Sandy a cup and settled next to Bear on the picnic table. "Now what's the big news?"

Sandy leaned forward and rested his elbows on his knees. "I'm retiring."

Candy felt Tyler tense behind her, but she relaxed. Somehow, she'd known this was coming the second she and Tyler had announced they were getting married. The look on Sandy's face was as if a weight had been lifted. His work, his real work, was done.

"No, you're not." Jason shook his head.

"Jason." Cassie swatted his leg.

"But you can't." Jason shoved her hand away.

"I can and I am. I had thirty years in teaching before I retired to manage you boys full time and we've had twenty years together. It's time." He took a drink from his coffee cup and set it aside. "You need newer, younger management. Like Candy."

Candy jerked upright spilling her wine all over her dress. "Dammit." She brushed at the wine. "Sandy, what are you taking about? I'm not a manager. I'm a publicist."

"You've got Tessa and Helen to back you up. At this point, it's a no-brainer anyway."

"Marc, why aren't you telling him he can't retire?" Jason demanded.

"Because I can't." Marc draped his arm around Alex's shoulders. "He's right. He's had two good careers and he's old."

"Thank you." Sandy sneered at Marc.

"You know what I mean, old man. I say take the retirement and enjoy it. Look at all the grandkids you get to play with." Marc gestured to the end of the yard. Then he tugged Alex tighter.

That was funny. Marc tugging Alex tighter. Candy sat up. So her dress was ruined. This was important. "Marc, are you trying to tell us something, too?"

"What would I be trying to tell you?"

"No way." Maureen stood up and pulled Alex to her feet. "I thought the five-year plan didn't include kids for another two years."

"Technically, by the time the baby is born we'll only be one year ahead of schedule." Alex grinned.

Maureen hugged her before Tessa could yank her into an embrace.

"Come on, babe. A nice even three," Jason said to Cassie.

"Oh, shut up." Cassie shoved him away and stood up to hug Alex.

Tyler kissed Candy's cheek. "What do you think about another trip to China?"

"I think I might be busy trying to learn to manage a bunch of spoiled rock stars." She patted Sandy's hand. "But I get to learn from one of the best."

"And you didn't think you were qualified." Sandy kissed her hand before standing to hug Alex himself.

Be sure not to miss Book 4.5 in Christa's Drawn to the Rhythm series

NOT SECOND BEST

No more solos for this heart...

As a lawyer at Touchstone management, Tessa's position brings her up close and personal to some of the world's biggest heartthrobs. Sometimes that intimacy crosses professional lines, which is understandable considering Tessa's impressive contact list. But when rock star Brian Ellis set her aside for the girl of his dreams, Tessa can't help wonder if Dzspinster auntdz is her true vocation. Which explains her hook-up with rising star Brett Cherney at Brian's celebrity wedding...

As the lead singer of BroRide, Brett has lived the rock-n-roll bad-boy lifestyle to the very hilt. But when the girl of his dreams marries fellow rocker Brian Ellis, he buries his disappointment in the arms of an older woman. The following morning, Brett realizes what he experienced was only the beginning of a song he's been trying to write all his life. It's a seductive theme, which Tessa falls for again and again, but getting her to believe they have a hit is turning out to be far from a sure thing...

A Lyrical Shine novella on sale now!

Learn more about Christa Maurice at http://www. kensingtonbooks.com/author.aspx/29516

Chapter 1

Tessa walked outside, maintaining her happy expression past the knot of smokers by the door. This wedding shouldn't bug her so much. Brian had gotten over his crush on her years ago. Shit, he'd been married before. She'd fallen off his pedestal a long time ago. So why did this marriage seem like the end of the world?

Suzi made a beautiful bride. One of her friends had designed the simple white gown for her. Ribbons of rainbow colors started as faint pastels across the bust and gained intensity as they wrapped around her body and down the back of her dress until they formed a brilliant train. Daisies wound through her upswept hair and complemented her pretty, sweet face. Brian looked rather sharp, too, in his white tux, open at the throat. His best accessory, though, had to be the expression of utter joy in his eyes.

It made Tessa want to puke. Not because they were happy. No, never that. Brian deserved to be happy. Suzi did, too. Apparently, everyone deserved to be happy.

Except her.

"Nice show, huh?"

Tessa glanced at Brett who'd wandered up beside her at the overlook. Or maybe she'd wandered up beside him. The ocean smashed into the cliffs below as if it held a grudge against her. "Yeah. They look really happy."

"She's the Holy Grail," Brett said. He leaned on the guardrail, fiddling a cigarette between his fingers. "She was a total mess when she left Logan last year. I took her out to this place I go to. Never laid a hand on her."

Tessa nodded. Why did he think she should care? Everybody knew he'd pulled Suzi out of the party where she'd broken up with her last boyfriend, Logan, nearly a year ago. Tessa had been one of many people trying to figure out where the hell they'd gone for weeks before Suzi had reappeared at Jason's West Virginia place. "You're a big damn hero."

"Something like that." He flicked the cigarette off the cliff, unlit. "Brian's a good guy, right? He'll be good to her, won't he?"

"I've known him since he was a kid. He'd walk through hell for her." Brian was the best guy. Absolute heart of gold. If she'd been half awake ten years ago, she could have had that.

"Good. That's good. Cause next time I have to haul her away from some asshole, I'm not going to be so easygoing about letting her leave."

"What the fuck are you talking about?" She glared at Brett, but he looked as if he'd been dragged backward through the desert by a tour bus, and she faltered. "What's wrong with you?"

Brett turned and stared at the ocean. "Probably the same thing that's wrong with you."

"What's that supposed to mean?"

"Oh, come on. How dumb do you think everybody is? You've known Brian since he was in elementary school. His daughter is named after you. The only person at this wedding who looks sicker about it is Logan." Brett bobbed his head. "And maybe me. You and Brian had a thing, or you wish you had a thing, or something. I'd say I could write a great song about it, but there's already been a bunch. Etta James did three or four."

"So, are you telling me that party-hearty Brett Cherney lost his poor little heart to the bride?" Tessa meant to smirk, but it came out twisted because of the sob she was trying to cover.

"Only as much as tough lawyer Tessa Callisto lost her heart to the groom."

Tessa stared in the direction of the pavilion. More than six hundred guests. This wedding was almost as well attended as the Grammys. No point hiring a band because no local band could hold a candle to this audience, so music had been supplied by a running jam. Everyone was having a blast. They wouldn't notice a couple of people missing. "You know what the best cure for a broken heart is, don't you?"

"What?" He glanced over his shoulder as if the answer to her question was back at the wedding reception.

She stared into Brett's eyes. Brett, who slept with every female who caught his fancy. And there were lots of those. What with his lean build and washboard abs, he was a good-looking specimen. "Wanna?" She arched an eyebrow at him.

His lips curled into a smile. "Sounds good to me."

"Your place or mine?"

"I'm thinking of some place more neutral."

* * * *

Brett slammed her against the door as soon as it was closed. All the way here, she'd been teasing him. Running her hand up the inside of his thigh, dragging her fingers through his hair, toying with his earlobe. And every time he'd reached for her, she'd smacked his hand away and told him to watch the road.

"Your ass is mine now," he growled, pressing his face into the curve of her neck.

"I was hoping you wanted more than that."

"Believe me. I plan to have every inch of you before I'm done."

Laughing, she ripped his shirt open and shoved it down his arms. "Let's see if you can deliver on that promise."

"I can." He hiked up her skirt. "Pantyhose? Really? These fucking things are like a force field around your sweet spot."

"I was going to the wedding of an old and dear friend, not headed out for a sleazy tryst."

"Damn." Brett dropped to his knees and pulled at the pantyhose. Her heavy, lusty scent crawled through his brain and straight into his dick. "I didn't think women wore these things anymore."

"I'm not the kind of woman you usually undress."

"No kidding." He smoothed his hands down her soft thighs, down to— "Your fucking shoes have buckles on the ankles. Is there a lock on your pussy, too?"

She laughed again. He glanced up in time to see her toss her blouse across the room. Underneath, she'd worn a lacy bra. Hopefully, it had a normal clasp and not some exotic thing like her goddamn shoes. He fumbled with the buckle, but his fingers couldn't grasp it.

"Let me help you." She crouched, pinned between the door and him, trying to reach her shoes through the tangle of pantyhose. Her dark hair brushed his cheek, and he shivered. Tessa was hot. Way hotter than he'd ever thought.

"Screw that." Brett wrapped his arm around her waist and swung her onto the floor. "I can get to all the parts I need."

She buried her hands in his hair, drawing him into a deep kiss. Her tongue delved into his mouth as she ground her hips against his.

The urgent need in her touch sizzled along his skin. "You're a hell of a woman," he said, dragging his lips down her chest to the thankfully simple front clasp on her bra.

"Thanks, now quit wasting time."

"You on a schedule?" He flicked open the bra and curved his hand around the warm flesh of her breast.

"No, I just have a lot of work for you. You need to get busy."

"I love a take-charge woman." Reaching into his pocket, he located a condom.

"Then you are going to love me." She grabbed his pants and opened them. "You have a rubber? If not, I have some in my purse."

"I got it." He climbed to his knees and ripped open the foil. "Glad to know you have some, too. Wouldn't want to run out."

"I'm pretty sure the desk would send up more if we asked. I'm surprised they didn't give you a gift basket of them when we checked in." She stretched her arms over her head, which did delightful things to her shape.

"I don't bring women here." Brett lifted her nylon-bound ankles over his head and crawled between her legs.

"Except me." Tessa licked her lips. "And Suzi."

Her and Suzi. Brett closed his eyes as he thrust into her, trying to imagine Suzi under him and only feeling Tessa's hot, sleek body and wet, soft mouth. He wrapped his arms around her, riding her hard and fast, lost in the wild rhythm of their bodies sliding together. Her legs clenched around his hips as if she'd never let him go. Beneath him, her eyes were closed and her mouth open as she gasped. Her dusky skin was slick with sweat.

His control slipped, and he groaned. "I don't think I can wait."

"You'll make it up to me." She tightened her hold on him, arching her hips to meet his.

He came in a heated satin rush, his whole body aching in the crest. Throughout, he could feel her arms and legs around him. Cradling him. For once, he didn't feel like he was in free fall. Funny, but he didn't hate the sensation the way he'd always thought he would. It was safety. Security. It was… "Tessa," he murmured.

"Just finish the job." She dug her fingernails into his back.

He thrust against her again until she came apart in his arms.

Sighing, she let her head loll on the carpet. "That was distracting."

"No problem." Brett swallowed his disappointment. Distracting? He'd never been called that before. The women he'd had lately had been a little more impressed. Fame was very impressive to a groupie. But Tessa was no groupie. She'd been in the thick of fame when he was still singing in the school holiday pageant. "Glad I could be of help."

"I hope I was just as distracting for you." She ruffled her fingers through his hair.

"Definitely." Brett slithered down her body and between her legs. She sat up as soon as she could and went to work on her shoes as if he wasn't even in the room. Okay, weird. Though he wasn't sure why it was so important she pay attention to him. He'd gotten what he wanted. He should be happy she didn't want to cuddle. Standing, he pulled his pants up. "I guess I'll take a shower."

"Go ahead, but I'm just going to get you dirty again." She didn't look up from her shoes.

"Good. I'll get really clean so you have to work harder." He went into the bathroom and turned on the water. Then he leaned on the door and listened to her walk around the other room.

The famous Jason Callisto's sister and lawyer, Tessa, had always been unattainable. She not only outclassed him in fame, but in brains, and at the reception had appeared totally together until she'd walked away. That was the reason he'd followed her. Because she'd stopped looking cool and started looking more like he felt. Except that just now, she'd been utterly chill.

Brett ducked under the water. He should have known better than to think he knew her this quickly. They had one stupid thing in common. Being second best.

But Tessa was a pretty awesome second.

The bathroom door opened. Tessa peeked around the shower door. "Mind if I join you?"

Brett stepped back to give her room. "You got the shoes off."

"They aren't difficult. They just defeated you." Smirking, she draped her arms around his shoulders.

"Ha, ha. I have some buckles that might defeat you." Brett let his hands slide down her sides with the flow of the water.

"I might let you try those out." She leaned on him, her skin velvet against his.

"I thought I'd distracted you enough."

"That was then. This is now."

"You're demanding."

"I think you can fulfill my demands." She picked up the soap and traced down his chest with it. "You were concerned about being dirty."

"You're not going to give me a chance to get clean, either." Brett studied her eyes, trying to figure out where she was going. Five minutes ago, she'd all but told him to get lost, and now, she was crawling all over him again.

"On the contrary, I'm going to clean you up." She rubbed the soap on a cloth and started sweeping the cloth across his chest. "How's that?"

"Nice."

"Take notes, because it's going to be your turn in a minute." The cloth dipped lower.

"I look forward to it." He did love a woman who knew what she wanted and wasn't afraid to spell it out.

"I'm sure you do," she purred. "You always were a show-off."

"What do you know about me?"

"Everything I need to." She stroked with the cloth along his length, which was very interested in the stimulation.

"Everything you need to?"

"You're a sleazy little party boy riding on the success of his first little hit and sleeping with every willing female you can find."

"You have no respect for me at all, do you?"

"I have lots of respect for you." She shifted him into the water to rinse him off and handed him the washcloth. "Right now I need a little party boy to fuck me thoroughly, and you are just the one to do it." Her breathing was heavy and slow.

"Thanks." He ran the cloth between her full breasts. She looked great naked. How old was she anyway? Jason was about forty. She must be a couple years older than her brother. Had he been overlooking an entire group of hot women because none of the chicks he'd picked was over thirty?

"Think nothing of it."

He soaped around her ass. Bigger than most of his girls', but tight and toned. Tessa had some substance to her. He slid between her legs from behind, drawing her against him and getting a sweet moan out of her. Her mouth curved into a lush smile.

"I knew you'd be frisky enough." Then she pulled away and rinsed off. "I've never heard of this place. How did you find it?"

"One of the guys my mom went with brought her here."

"Oh?" Tessa lifted her hair and rolled her neck under the hot water. "She was a backup singer, wasn't she?"

"Yeah."

"OD'd about ten years ago?"

"How did you know?"

Opening her eyes, she turned off the water. "My job is to know things."

"About me?" Brett followed her out of the shower. He'd thought he went after her at the reception, but maybe it was the other way around. She was smart. Maybe she'd lured him outside.

"When you and Suzi took off together, Jason had me hunting you. Best place to start looking was your past. Your dad is a nice guy." She walked from the bathroom, still dripping.

"My dad?"

"I called him trying to find you. So how did you end up being the guy to rescue Suzi?" She shoved open the patio door and stepped outside.

"Right place, right time."

Tessa cocked an eyebrow at him. "And she just ran off with you."

"When we were on tour, I got to know her, and I happened to be right there when she needed to leave." Brett hoped the heat on his face was sun and not embarrassment.

"You wanted to get next to her."

"Fuck yes, I did." Blushing. Definitely. "With a nickname like Randy Mirandy and a hot bod like hers, who wouldn't?"

"Indeed." Tessa stepped into the infinity pool and settled where she could stare out over the desert.

Brett clambered into the water next to her. This place was his refuge. After he'd come here with Suzi, it had also been his place to regret. He'd spent hours soaking in this pool, wondering what kind of moron he'd been to let Suzi get away and if there had been anything he could have done to stop it. "What about you? You knew Brian since he was a kid. He was married before. Why's it a crisis now?"

Tessa lifted one leg, put it down, and lifted the other, pointing her toe at the sky before lowering it into the water. "Brian had a huge crush on me when he was a kid. Well, up until he was about twenty-two, but I wasn't interested."

"So now you want what some other chick has?"

"No," Tessa snapped, glaring at him. "It's just an ego blow that he's not going to be following me around anymore."

"Right. Because he was before."

"Fuck you."

"In a little bit. I'm comfortable now."

Tessa slouched in the corner. "I just can't believe all those guys got married like that. Bear and Maureen. Jason and Cassie. Marc and Alex. Now Brian and Suzi. Another one bites the dust. I've known all those guys since we were kids."

"Ty's not hitched up yet."

"He's probably meeting his one true love as we speak. I'll be running background checks on her tomorrow. My mother is dating a guy from Cassie's hometown. Connie's even dating."

"Who's Connie?"

"My sister."

"Everybody's married but you."

"I don't want to be married," she growled.

Brett held up his hands. "Hey, don't look at me. I'm not looking for a wife here, either." He eased into the water. "I love this place."

"It's nice. Very relaxing. What made you bring Suzi here?"

"I knew a shitload of people would be hunting for her, and she needed some time away. Nobody would look for her here."

"This where she had her miscarriage?"

"Yeah."

"That must have been rough."

"I took care of her." Brett shrugged. He'd stood outside the bathroom door, fretting about what to do. She hadn't wanted him to call a doctor, but she'd been in so much pain. Then she'd cried all night. Holding her and not being able to do a damn thing to help her had sucked, but it had been better than standing outside a door.

"She's one of those women who doesn't have babies easily. Brian's already got the two, so he doesn't care," Tessa said.

"Do we have to talk about Brian all the time?"

"I thought that's why we were here. Because we both came in second."

"Then maybe we should call Logan. He came in second, too."

Tessa shrugged. "Go ahead if you want to, but I'm over my orgy phase. You two have fun. You can sit around and talk about how perfect Suzi is."

"Suzi's really nice." Brett scowled. Suzi was nice. Really friendly and approachable. Every time she'd joined them on the road when his band was touring with her ex's band, she'd found time to sit and talk, even though Logan had wanted her chained to his wrist whenever he was offstage. Tessa could be as bitchy as she wanted, but she'd better not start talking shit about Suzi.

"I know. She's a great girl. Always has been. Did you know she tried to patch up Brian and Bonnie's marriage? I could have told her it was a waste of time."

Brett couldn't decide which was worse. Talking about Brian or talking about Suzi. "I'm hungry. I'm going to order some dinner. You want anything?"

Tessa frowned at the desert. "Rum and Coke. Steak, well done. Baked potato, butter, no sour cream. Steamed summer squash. And chocolate frosting."

"Frosting without the cake?"

She smiled at him. "It's for later."

Brett grinned back. At least if she was going to torture him by talking about Brian and Suzi, she would make up for it.

Meet the Author

Christa Maurice has been obsessed with rock stars from early childhood when her older brother started randomly quizzing her on rock trivia. How many first graders knew who the headliners were on the Black and Blue Tour? Christa did. (Black Sabbath and Blue Oyster Cult.) When not listening to music and/or writing, she enjoys traveling, reading and science fiction. Keep Coming Back To Love is the sixth book in her Drawn to the Rhythm Romance series. Readers can find Christa on Facebook or visit her website at christamaurice.com. Sign up for her newsletter here: http://eepurl.com/bQrDN5.